Guns of
Santa Carmelita

Hugh Martin

A Black Horse Western

ROBERT HALE · LONDON

© Anthony A. Glynn 2016
First published in Great Britain 2016

ISBN 978-0-7198-1804-2

Robert Hale Limited
Clerkenwell House
Clerkenwell Green
London EC1R 0HT

www.halebooks.com

Printed and bound in Great Britain by
CPI Antony Rowe, Chippenham and Eastbourne

Guns of Santa Carmelita

When the former deputy town marshal, Frank Calland, helps out another saddle-tramp whom he finds stranded without food or water in the Arizona desert, he doesn't know what he is getting himself into.

Before he knows it, Calland is being pursued by an angry posse. This is only the beginning of Calland's dramas. Once again he finds himself donning the lawman's star as deputy to Marshal Bill Riggs, who seems to be hiding a dark secret from his past.

Calland is thrown into the deep end and must take responsibility when Jay Seaton's band of ruthless outlaws arrives in the town of Santa Carmelita. Fresh from the recent war, they are bloodthirsty for revenge.

CHAPTER ONE

HOT LEAD PURSUIT

Yet another bullet fanned past Frank Calland's right ear with an angry *whang*, coming close to biting a chunk out of it. Calland ducked and almost buried his nose in the tossing mane of his horse. He was riding flat out with one hand grasping the reins and the other filled with a bucking .45 Colt, spitting unsighted shots back at the posse, following on drumming hoofs.

'Goddamn it—the next shot will likely finish me!' he growled to himself as he tried to spur-rake more speed out of his lathered bronc.

He twisted his head to look back and, through a swirling curtain of hoof-risen Arizona grit, he could make out that he had increased some of the distance between himself and the doggedly pursuing riders. He spurred harder.

A portion of his mind detached itself from the sweaty welter of panicky haste to wonder why these townsmen of Stone Creek City were on his tail when he knew not one man jack of them and he had never been in their town before....

Calland rode into Stone Creek City's single street, a saddle tramp who hoped he might find work in this desert-edge ranching country. He was accompanied by the man who said his name was Beale, to all appearances as much a saddle tramp as himself, whom he met on the trail something like an hour before reaching the town.

He knew nothing about Beale and did not particularly take to him. He had a bland, immobile face which seemed to hold a kind of innocence but this was offset by his darkly brooding eyes.

Beale was almost out of water in harsh, inhospitable and sun-punished country. He said he had not eaten properly in nearly two days—so Calland did the only thing a man could do on encountering one in such distress in that kind of terrain. He shared both his canteen and some of his meagre supply of grub with him. Thereafter, Beale strung along with Calland.

Calland did not know why Beale was headed for Stone Creek City. Nor did he particularly care. Beale was of the kind who did not go in for gab. Calland quickly noted that his trail companion hardly ever initiated a conversation. He mostly spoke when spoken to and then with great economy of words. He would ride in silence for long stretches.

Soon after they met, Calland asked him if he knew Stone Creek City and if he had ever been there before.

'Once, some time back,' said Beale.

'I hear tell a good many of these desert edge ranchers gather there. A man might run into one needing hands for the upcoming spring round-up.'

'He might. You never know.'

Calland and Beale almost never knew what hit them within five minutes of arriving on Stone Creek City's main street. They rode past plank walks bearing sparse citizenry. In towns in these climes that were little more than huddled clusters of clapboard and adobe buildings, many folk took a siesta around noon. The brassy sun could blaze uncomfortably even this early in spring.

Suddenly, there was an incoherent hoot followed by a harsh voice, yelling almost hysterically, 'Hey! It's one of Jay Seaton's gang! One of those who killed Seth Cooper! I was in the bank and I saw it!'

A man stood on a plank walk close to Calland and Beale, with his arm flung out and his finger pointing at Beale. As soon as he voiced the alarm, he scooted back and crouched behind a barrel in front of a store. Then a second man appeared from a store, looked at the horsemen briefly. His mouth dropped open.

'By God—he's right! He's the one whose mask slipped as the gang left the bank. He's one of that murdering crew, all right!' His raucous voice was carried along the street like an alarm.

The man disappeared into the store but reappeared almost at once, flourishing a rifle.

Beale was white-faced. He grabbed for the Colt holstered at his hip, hauled it from leather at the same time, spurring his horse.

'Get the hell out!' he barked at Calland.

Though bewildered, Calland needed no second bidding. Abruptly, the street seemed to be alive with men bearing firearms and running for hitched horses. He and Beale punished their animals, riding like the wind, raising the dust and travelling the whole length of the solitary street.

Behind them came a hastily formed scratch posse, riding with a tenacious determination and now and again loosing wild shots. The main street became the trail, winding off to the far line of tawny hills, shimmering behind the heat haze. Beyond them lay Mexico....

Calland tried to urge more speed out of his bronc but he knew the animal had already put in a tough spell of desert travel and was not capable of much more. He looked behind him again and realized that, abruptly, they were gone. As a sigh of relief gusted out of him, it came to him that his erstwhile pursuers were men who lived settled, town-bound lives. They were store owners or their employees who worked behind counters; well-fed citizens, many with hefty paunches.

None were used to a hard life in the saddle. Furthermore, some were probably mounted on horses that were not their own, animals belonging to others, grabbed in alarm from the hitch-rails on the street. At all events, they had quit the chase.

He slackened his bronc's speed and, with his eyes, searched the thick haze of dust behind him. He gasped on finding that Beale had totally disappeared.

Had he stopped one of their bullets, so the pursuers gave up the chase because Beale was the one they were after?

Calland remembered passing a stand of stunted, spindly trees to one side of the trail, as near a forest as might be found in this dried-out country. If Beale had plunged his horse into them in the hope of losing the townsmen among them, it was a desperate and forlorn hope. Such trees offered very little in the way of cover. On the other hand, he might have intended to abandon Calland, dismount, speedily position himself behind a tree and snipe at any riders who followed him.

Not that Calland cared particularly about Beale. The pair had met by chance and Calland was pretty sure he would never consciously seek Beale's company. He did not have the look of a desirable trail-partner. If he had fallen victim to the men from Stone Creek City and it was due to mistaken identity, it was a tragedy.

Calland remembered the yells concerning a man being killed in what sounded like a raid on a bank.

If Beale was guilty and was fool enough to return to a town where the citizenry hankered after justice and were determined to deal it out with hot lead, he'd been a damned fool.

It was safe enough to let the bronc take the trail at its own pace and Calland slowed it to a walk over the pock-marks of hoofs and ruts of wheels in the harsh sand. This end of Arizona was new to Calland and he wondered where this trail eventually led. Possibly, it wended all the way to the distant line of hills and on through them into the state of Sonora in Mexico.

There were vistas of semi-desert on either side, with scattered boulders and tall, long-armed cacti standing like sentinels at intervals and when he rounded a twist in the trail, Calland found the land to his right shelved downward. Below the slope, there was a shining stretch of water. Beside it there was a margin of green.

This must be the creek after which Stone Creek City was named. His heart lifted. The prospect of water and graze on the creek bottoms for his weary horse was like manna from heaven.

He turned the bronc on to the downward slanting land. Smelling the water, the animal hastened its own pace down the slope and Calland tried to remember how much grub he had left after sharing some with Beale and he wondered if he was far enough from Stone Creek City to be totally safe from its vengeful citizenry.

He reckoned he had just enough food in his warsack to make a Spartan overnight camp, so he could give the bronc a lengthy rest and allow it to fill itself with the lush graze found on the creek bottoms.

He halted and climbed down from the saddle, allowing the bronc to walk on to the slowly flowing creek, drink and then begin cropping the green fronds of grass growing alongside the water.

Calland stretched his legs, eased the cricks in his back and joined the animal at the water's edge. He took his canteen from his saddle gear, filled it and took a drink. The water was in no way brackish and, after his recent, dust-choked exertions, Calland found it as satisfying as a choice wine.

He divested the bronc of its saddle and trappings and humped them up the slope to a promising spot sheltered by an outcropping of rock and some cactus growths. It was the sort of place where a man might settle down for the night and see what waited a little further along the trail the next day.

He certainly would not return to Stone Creek City, even if he learned the place was stiff with ranchers wanting take on new riders for the spring round

He realized that time was galloping along and it soon would be so far into round-up season that his chances of a job may already have passed.

With his bedroll spread under the shelter of the rock, he passed the night in a solid sleep after the wildly hectic exertions of the day, even though his supper was a sparse quantity of beef jerky and some bread—all that was left in his pack.

In the morning, both he and his horse were refreshed and they resumed the trail with energy, though Calland had no idea where it would lead them.

They were in plain sight of the hills when he spotted a haze of blue smoke, the sure clue of the many domestic smokestacks of a town. The emptiness in his innards and the prospect of eatables made him spur the bronc to a quicker pace.

He soon saw the town, the usual border collection of wooden and antique white adobe buildings indicating that this settlement dated from the time when this part of Arizona belonged to Mexico. He passed a slanted, sun-warped wooden sign which read: *Santa Carmelita*.

Soon, he was riding into a straggling street which was beginning to come to life. There were a handful of people around and a few hitched horses and wagons. Such a town was often tortured by searing heat and no one ever hurried. Calland halted the bronc and looked around.

He saw a lean, middle-aged man with a clipped moustache leaning against the wooden upright support of an awning over the far plank walk. He had a Colt Peacemaker revolver riding low on his right hip.

Wearing a six-shooter in that style betokened

gun-slinging competence and the man's bronzed face, hard and unsmiling, suggested he would be a tough proposition to tangle with. He watched Calland studying the stores and businesses along the plank walks on both sides of the street.

The chief consideration on Calland's mind at that moment was finding a restaurant where he could eat at moderately low cost.

After a short time, the watching man straightened up from his leaning position and began to walk across the street towards Calland. The sun put a sparkle on a detail that was obscured when he was leaning on the upright—a lawman's star on his buckskin vest.

I might have known it, thought Calland. Only a lawman would take that kind of interest in a stranger in a town like this, so close to the Mexican border. Many a joker whose face is on a wanted poster might come through. From his own experience, he had reason to understand a law officer's anxieties about strangers who showed up within his jurisdiction.

The man with the badge walked right up to Calland and nodded to him.

'Howdy. You looking for anyone in particular?' he asked.

'No, but I'm wondering if you have any big scale ranches hereabout where a man might be taken on for the round-up.'

'There's only one really big outfit around here, Bart

Sawyer's Box BS, but I reckon you're a mite late for the round-up crew.... Wait, here's a man who'll know for sure.' He waved to a heavily built man in range gear, crossing the street a short distant away and called, 'Hey, Hank, come over here for a minute.'

The bulky man strode up to them and eyed Calland.

'This is Hank Taylor, the Box BS foreman,' said the lawman. 'Hank, this young fellow wants to know if there's any chance of joining your round-up crew.'

Under his broad-brimmed sombrero, Taylor pulled a gloomy face. 'Nothing doing, Bill, we've taken on all we need and we start rounding-up tomorrow, a few days late. Up to last evening, we were short-handed. Then three fellows showed up looking for work. Mr Sawyer signed 'em on and said we now had all the crew we need. And I know all the smaller outfits are fully manned and are already rounding up.' He turned to Calland. 'Sorry, stranger. Pity you didn't come to town this time yesterday.'

Calland shrugged. 'Can't be helped,' he said, trying to sound more nonchalant than he felt.

Hank Taylor gave him an amiable nod. 'Good luck, wherever you go from here,' he said and then resumed his walk across the street.

The man with the badge looked at Calland with a shrewd gaze. 'I'm Bill Riggs, town marshal here,' he said. "Where'd you come from?'

'Before hitting Arizona a few days ago, I was up

in Boulder Pass in Indian Territory, on the edge of Arkansas.'

Marshal Bill Riggs's eyebrows rose. 'Boulder Pass is Tom Clafford's town. His reputation as a town tamer is pretty darned near nation-wide. As a town marshal there's no man to touch him.'

'You don't have to tell me,' Calland smiled. 'I was his deputy.'

The lawman's brows lifted a little higher. 'You were? Why'd you leave? Weren't fired, were you?'

'No. I quit, though Marshal Clafford wanted me stay on.'

'Well, if Clafford wanted you to stay on, you must have suited him and if you suited Tom Clafford, you must have been tolerably good.'

'I did the job to the best of my ability and Marshal Clafford never complained. But I just got the wander-lust. Got a notion I'd like to ride the range again. I guess it's in my blood. I started out as a kid and, hard as it is, I like it. I've been getting attacks of wanderlust now and again ever since I left the army.'

'Army?'

'Yes. I did a fair hitch in the cavalry. I spent a long time in New Mexico. I was in the Yellow Hoof outbreak, under Colonel Shattock.'

Marshal Bill Riggs blew out his cheeks. 'Then you saw some action. As a fighting Indian, Yellow Hoof was some proposition.'

Calland gave a slight, ironic smile. 'I'll say he was. If the tribes ever had a West Point Academy for fighting Indians, Yellow Hoof would be in charge of it.'

Hunger pains were beginning to nag at his innards and he shifted restlessly in the saddle. 'Look, Marshal, where can I get a solid meal?' he asked.

The lawman pointed up the street. 'Up yonder, on your left, you'll see Dave Cox's eating house. The grub's good. Tell Dave the marshal highly recommended him and mebbe he'll put some extra on your plate.'

Calland gathered his rein, ready to move off. 'Thanks, Marshal Riggs. I'm obliged to you.'

'Hey, hold hard for a moment,' said the lawman. 'How'd you like the job of deputy right here in Santa Carmelita? I figure you're right well qualified for it and I have the power to swear you in here and now if you're willing.'

Calland looked at him, surprised. Feeling a rush of gratitude to the law officer, he said: 'Why, sure. If I can't get a place on a round-up crew, I'm over a barrel. I gladly accept, Marshal.'

Riggs held him in his unwavering gaze. He said levelly, 'You must understand you're offered the job on condition that you don't give in to wanderlust and quit all over again. I need a deputy because the one I had got itchy feet, which seems to be an epidemic among you younger folk—like whiskey, cards and chasing women.

'Harry Schultz was his name. He was a good man

16

until he got wind of a gold-rush, back yonder, in Mexico. He felt the urge to quit his job, pack kit and caboodle and go after the gold.

'I told him I saw men who hazed off on a gold panic half a dozen times. Some abandoned homes, wives and kids and never returned laden with gold. Some never returned at all. But he wouldn't listen. The deputy's badge is yours provided you stick with the job. What's your name, by the way?'

'Frank Calland—and I'll stick with the job.'

'OK. Go and eat. My office is right opposite the eating house. Take your horse to the yard in back of the office before you eat. There's a stable there, with a water trough and some feed. Come into the office after your meal and I'll deputize you.'

Calland found his way to the marshal's office and its yard and watered his bronc at the trough there. In the stable, there was a docile chestnut roan, presumably the lawman's mount, in a stall, and a supply of feed.

He divested his bronc of saddle and trappings, then backed the animal into a second, empty stall and left it feeding there.

Over at the eating house, Dave Cox proved to be a plump man with mutton chop whiskers adorning a jovial countenance. The restaurant was empty of customers and Cox, whose ample middle suggested he liked his food, was behind his counter, leaning forward on it, and watching Calland with interest as he entered.

He nodded as Calland strode up to the counter.

'Mr Cox? Marshal Riggs heartily recommends your establishment as the best restaurant in Santa Carmelita.'

'He does, does he?' Cox replied with a rumbling chuckle. 'That's right good of him and he knows what he's talking about—he eats here himself often enough.' He paused, chuckled again and added, ''Course, he ain't got much choice but to recommend my place since it's the only eatery in town! What can I do for you?'

'I'd like something solid. I've travelled some on hard rations for a long time.'

'I figure I can fill that bill to fill the spaces in a trail-hungry man,' said Cox. 'Seems to me beef, potatoes, three vegetables and hot coffee are called for. And how about topping it off with a slice of the apple pie my wife bakes? There are folks hereabouts who'd walk barefoot through the snow to eat my Evelina's apple pie—that's if we ever had any snow to speak of in these parts.'

'It all sounds just right,' said Calland. He liked the look of Dave Cox. His broad, good natured face, his chuckle and his amiable line of chat signalled a totally genuine personality.

The food was not long in being served and Calland was faced with a heaped plate of appetizing fare and a pot of strong coffee.

As he ate, Dave Cox continued his conversation from his post behind the counter. 'So you've met our town marshal,' he commented. 'Bill Riggs is a damned fine lawman. The best Santa Carmelita ever had and it needs a tough man to keep order here. Being within a hoot and a holler of the Mexican border, we've had our share of hard cases passing through in the past.

'More recently, with a supposed gold strike over in Mexico, we've had a different type of saddle-pilgrim showing up—the kind attracted by gold. I guess a good many are just hopefuls who're dumb enough to imagine they'll strike pay-dirt right off and become millionaires overnight. Others are probably the dangerous kind: the cut-throats and barefaced robbers who infest every gold-camp.

'They all came here to eat and you'd have a hell of a job sorting one kind from the other. Marshal Riggs made it pretty plain he would not put up with any lawlessness.' He paused, looking at Calland thoughtfully, as if expecting him to comment.

Seeing that Calland was too busy eating, he resumed. 'He came in here one night when there were a bunch of new arrivals eating. I have to admit they were good for business. The marshal made a speech and told these jokers he was tolerant and willing to let them trade at the town's stores, eat here and drink in the saloons but he'd have no drunkenness, brawling, shooting or any other kind of deviltry.

'Well, all was peaceable and they got out of town next morning. I guess all had some inkling of the marshal's reputation and would not put him to the test.'

Calland looked up from his meal. 'Reputation?' he queried sharply.

'Sure, Marshal Riggs is known all along this border country as an honest, tough and straight-shooting lawman. And he sure can shoot straight when there's call for it. There's few who can match him in a gunfight. He never says much about himself but he's built up a reputation bigger than those supposed heroes they write dime novels about,' said Cox.

Calland laid down his cup and sat back.

'Well, that makes good hearing because he's fixing to swear me in as his deputy, right after I finish this pleasant meal,' he said, pouring himself a fresh cup of coffee.

'He is? He must think you have what takes. Got any previous experience?'

'Sure. I used to be deputy to Marshal Tom Clafford over at Boulder Pass in Indian Territory.'

Cox's eyes widened. 'That's impressive, I don't have to tell you that Clafford's name is known to pretty well every man-jack west of the Mississippi. I'm darned glad to know this town looks like having a couple of top-notch lawmen for the near future.

'Bill Riggs could keep a tight lid on things when he was on his own. But, with that gold rush going on in

Mexico, bringing all manner of riff-raff to this end of Arizona, it's good to know his arm is strengthened by a good deputy. I have a hunch that Santa Carmelita will yet have its share of trouble.'

CHAPTER TWO

RETURN OF THE LOST ONE

Paso Jacinto was nobody's idea of paradise. A fly-blown hiding hole just inside Mexico, it was a place of abandonment that had once, long ago, had some importance. It was now a sprawling collection of crumbling adobe buildings littering the desert, a forgotten ghost town.

Its population regularly fluctuated but usually had a good contingent of locally grown outlaws and vagabonds and ruffians from the United States, who rode the owl hoot trail and needed to go to ground for a spell or perhaps for good and all.

The ramshackle law-enforcement mechanism had sparse sway in Paso Jacinto, and the wide variety of fugitives and adventurers from over the border who showed up in the town had little to fear from that quarter.

A villainous collection of border drifters had appeared in Paso Jacinto since gold was struck in the

Jacinto River region nearby. Reports of how magnificent the strike was varied but none were ever played down. All the tales had it that every adventurer who went in search of the precious metal struck a fortune in no time at all.

Where there was even the smell of fortune the scene was likely to be very soon invaded by claim-jumpers, spurious assay agents, confidence tricksters, cunningly clever thieves and downright brutal thieves.

Jay Seaton and his gang of bank robbers had scooted over the border and holed up in Paso Jacinto immediately after hitting the bank in Stone Creek City. Seaton was a lean and scarred string-bean of a man who had never thrown off the persona of a guerrilla commander which he took on when quite young and in the Confederate army. Units such as his earned reputations of such infamy that the Southern government eventually took pains to deny that they were a legitimate part of the army.

He never ditched his old wartime habits with the coming of peace and his equally diehard riders were the scourge of several states and territories of the expanding frontier for almost the full decade since the Civil War ended.

Seaton drilled his raiders in what he considered intelligent techniques in bank robbery: to know exactly where in town a bank was situated; what its interior layout was; how many people it employed and where their work stations were. It was also desirable to know the quickest exit from town and the strength of the local forces of law and the position of the office of the sheriff or town marshal in relation to the bank.

Preparations called for careful spying some days before the event by a member of the gang who could enter town as an inconspicuous visitor, survey the inside of the bank on entering with some minor inquiry. Seaton never mounted a raid without first making a preparatory survey.

The raid itself should always be unexpected, swiftly executed with every man knowing his role and everyone masked by a bandanna covering the lower face. The escape should be made just as swiftly. Seaton's careful planning kept casualties on either side down to a minimum but they did occur and the Seaton outfit had scattered its back trail with a dozen or more wanted posters. Many splashed dramatic and lurid accounts of the capital crime of murder.

The raid on the bank in Stone Creek City was a case in point. Just as it started, with the masked raiders inside the building, a young teller had hauled a shotgun from under his desk and Cal Daggett, the most impetuous of Seaton's gang, immediately shot him dead. The escape made by the raiding horsemen, pounding out of town directly towards the border, was accomplished quickly—but not faultlessly.

When well out of Stone Creek City and with time

to reflect on the raid, it was found that Cal Daggett, who had just boosted the murder score of the Seaton bunch, was missing.

Three days after the Stone Creek City robbery, Dan Forrest, a heavily bearded, pugnacious faced member of Seaton's gang, was sitting on a rock in the yard of the abandoned house the gang was occupying. In the torpid heat with the sun blazing against a faultless blue sky, Forrest was trying to make the most of the slight shade of a sun-spilt tree and smoking a cigarillo when a weary man trudged through the yard's crumbling gateposts. He led a horse, jaded by travel and lean through inadequate feeding.

Forrest's mouth fell open and he snatched the smoke from his lips at the sight of the man and animal. He stood up suddenly.

'Daggett! Hell, we figured you were dead!' he exclaimed.

The new arrival trudged towards him. 'I ain't dead—just all-in. I need water, and so does the cayuse. The both of us are pretty well dried up.'

Forrest nodded to a pump and a trough in a far corner of the yard. 'Water over yonder,' he said. 'What in hell happened to you and where have you been?'

'Let's just say I got lost,' retorted Daggett curtly as he neared the inviting source of water.

'I'll tell Jay you're here,' Forrest said and he started to walk towards the house.

The interior of the decayed adobe building was gloomy and thick with harsh tobacco smoke mixed with the strong smell of tamales being prepared in a neighbouring room. Jay Seaton's thin frame was sprawled along a battered old couch and various members of his crew of robbers were loafing here and there, smoking and dozing.

Forrest strode in out of the blazing sunshine, stood under the lintel of the door and announced, 'Daggett just showed up!'

Jay Seaton's skinny body jerked as though suddenly given an electric shock and he stood up.

'Where's he been?' he rasped at Forrest. His voice had a markedly Southern inflexion.

Forrest shrugged. 'He didn't say. He just said he got lost.'

Daggett appeared and stood in the doorway, backing Forrest's bulky frame and wiping his mouth with the back of his hand, after drinking copiously from the pump.

'How'd you get lost, you damned fool?' growled Seaton. 'You should have stuck with the rest of us when we lit out of town after hitting the bank.'

The chief of the gang was annoyed because it seemed one of his carefully plotted criminal ventures could have suffered because one of the raiders had, as the raider put it, lost himself.

It was not that any harm was done, but Seaton,

the old wartime chief of galloping guerrillas, had the pride of a general in his precise plotting of campaigns. That pride had been badly dented. A further murder had been added to the gang's tally and the smoothness of the strike had suffered through Daggett seeming to become lost.

Cal Daggett was careful to conceal a good deal of the truth when he related his experiences to Seaton in a breathless narrative.

'I did stick with the rest of you when you lit out,' he said defensively. 'But my horse suddenly went lame and I thought he'd thrown a shoe. He slowed down just as the whole damned town was running around, shouting about the bank raid and yelling for a posse to be got up, but he hadn't thrown a shoe. It was just that something spooked him. Maybe it was all the panic on the street. The rest of you had disappeared and I had to do something quick.

'Somehow in all that excitement, I wasn't spotted as I rode like hell between a couple of buildings and into an alley. I rode along the alley, back of the main street stores, to the end of town, then on to the desert and kept going until I was well clear of the town.'

Jay Seaton snorted as if he was not wholly satisfied with Daggett's yarn. 'You knew we were headed for Mexico. Why didn't you ride the desert until you struck the Mexico trail and come after us?'

'It wasn't that easy, Jay. The horse kept acting up,

whatever spooked him bothered him and he tried a couple of times to throw me. I had to calm him and find some way of watering him and resting him. I also had to watch out for parties from Stone Creek City beating around the desert, looking for our boys.'

Seaton snorted again and looked at Daggett suspiciously. 'Seems to me you got yourself to the other end of the town—the end we went in from and not the end we came out of, the Mexico end. It looks plumb stupid to me. I don't know why you thought anyone would search that side of the city. They knew we ran out of the other side.'

Growing in Seaton's mind was the suspicion that Daggett had the intention of deserting but thought better of it, knowing that to keep with the gang meant he had the relative security of numbers where, if alone, he would be vulnerable in a country alerted by the Stone Creek City raid.

Daggett swallowed and blamed his horse again. 'Sure, Jay, but it happened by accident. I was trying to get a panicky cayuse to calm down. What with his prancing around, and all, I didn't know what way he was heading when we scooted down the alley.'

He went to embroider a colourful tale of finding a waterhole on the desert where he and the horse rested up for a day and a half until riding south, circumventing Stone Creek City and finding the trail into Mexico.

He was desperate to keep some salient facts from

Seaton. One was that he was scared almost witless in the aftermath of the raid. His bandana slipped from his face while exiting the bank. Jay Seaton and the rest of the gang seemed not to have noticed it, all being busy mounting their animals at top speed to clear out of town. Daggett was pretty sure that someone among the panicking townsmen must have spotted his face.

Into the bargain, he was determined to keep his mouth shut about being helped out on the desert by a young saddle tramp who gave him water and food. He told this stranger he was called Beale, a false name he had used in lawless escapades long before.

And under no circumstances did he intend to admit he was fool enough to take his courage in both hands and return to Stone Creek City with the stranger in a bid to reach the trail to Mexico quickly. He kept Seaton in the dark about being recognized in the town and how he and his companion were chased by the hastily raised posse of townsmen.

In the pursuit, Cal Daggett plunged his horse into the stand of straggling trees, fully expecting at least some of the posse to follow him but, when he had zigzagged into the thick of the trees, he realized he was not pursued. Possibly, the fat and out of condition townsmen, many riding other peoples' horses, were too timid to risk a chase through such a hazardous location but that was a further facet of the tale he kept to himself.

Seaton glowered at Daggett. He knew it was he who shot the teller and half-suspected he had deliberately cut loose from the gang to go solo and hole up in some location far distant from the scene of the shooting.

'You should have held your nerve when that teller grabbed the shotgun,' Seaton said harshly.

'Hell, he could have blasted the whole bunch of us, Jay.'

'You don't know what kind of nerve he had. He could have realized he was surrounded by our guns and wouldn't risk a shot. You put all our necks into a noose when you fired, you damned fool.'

Daggett tried an ill-advised attempt at gallows humour. 'Well it'll only be one more noose among many already waiting for us, Jay,' he said.

'That's no consolation,' snarled Seaton. 'We're all under the shadow of the hangman's rope but there's no call to remind anyone of it.'

He jerked his head towards a door in a far corner. 'Go into the other room. Nebraska Carlsen is in there, handling the grub. He'll give you something to eat.'

Previously, Seaton had some faith in Daggett's stability. With his bland face which was unlikely to be well remembered, he had proved successful in spying out the prospects of a town and in entering a bank, posing as an innocent inquirer to survey its layout.

But after his uncharacteristic jittery action in shooting the teller in their last raid, Seaton wondered if it was going to pieces and he was losing his nerve.

He wondered, too, if his tale of getting lost after the raid did not cover an attempt to desert the gang of which he eventually thought better. The last thing Seaton wanted was any member cutting loose from the outfit and falling into the hands of questioning law officers.

Seaton watched Daggett's back disappear through the far door.

'Damned fool!' he muttered again.

CHAPTER THREE

A STAR FOR CALLAND

In the marshal's office in Santa Carmelita, Marshal Bill Riggs pinned the deputy marshal's star to Frank Calland's vest. Calland raised his right hand and repeated after the law officer the oath to protect and administer the constitution, laws and statutes of the United States of America and those of the Territory of Arizona.

'Now you're sworn in, I just hope you don't get that wanderlust fever again and go charging off to Mexico to hunt for gold,' said the marshal.

Calland grinned. 'No chance of it, Marshal. I've met enough disillusioned former prospectors to know chances of finding a fortune are pretty rare.'

Riggs nodded. 'I reckon you have horse-sense enough to know when you're well off. Where are you going to bed down?'

'Never thought about it but you tell me I'll draw

a good wage from the town council so I guess I can afford a rooming house here in town.'

'You can, but there's a place right here in the office you can have rent free,' Riggs said. 'My old deputy, Harry Schultz, bunked there and found it comfortable enough. It's through that door yonder. Of course, it's right next to the cells. We might have a noisy drunk in the jug, sometimes even a couple of 'em but I reckon you won't be kept awake too often.'

Calland followed Riggs through the door at the far end of the office and found a neat little room with a small but comfortable looking bed, a bedside table, a chair and a closet where clothes might be kept. Calland was impressed, thinking that a man might make himself at home in the little room.

'It's a sight better than the accommodation in most ranch bunkhouses,' said Calland.

'Sure is and, since I guess you have no gear other than what you wear on your back and carry in your saddle bags, you'll have no trouble moving in,' Riggs said.

Calland thanked him, relieved at how quickly and dramatically his fortunes had changed since he rode into Santa Carmelita.

'Come along and take a turn on the street,' the marshal invited. 'I want to introduce you to the mayor and some of the folks such as our storekeepers and some of your other neighbours who ought to know who you are.

'I also want to call at the telegraph office to see if any fresh news has come through.

'The Jay Seaton bunch has been active at this end of the border country for the first time. They raided a bank over at Stone Creek City, took a big haul and shot a bank worker dead.'

As if a bucket of cold water had unexpectedly been thrown over him, Calland was hit by the chilling memory of the hectic events immediately before his chance arrival in Santa Carmelita.

'Hell, Marshal, I guess I didn't have time to tell you. Everything happened so fast since I hit town, but I ran into one of the Jay Seaton gang just before I arrived here, fellow named Beale. I met him by chance on the desert.'

'Beale?' asked Riggs. He looked hard at Calland with narrowed eyes and asked again, 'Did you say Beale? Are you sure his name was Beale?'

'Yes. He was out of water and grub and on the far side of Stone Creek City. I helped him out and we rode into Stone Creek City together. Soon as we arrived there, somebody hollered that he knew Beale was one of the bank robbers of a short time before and the pair of us had to hit a real smart lick out of the town with half the citizens on our tails and shooting.'

He went on to relate the rest of the story, telling of the ultimate disappearance of Beale.

Bill Riggs considered him with his steady glare. 'You aren't feeding me with some wild yarn, are you?' he asked. 'You aren't handing me a tale to cover yourself in any way? You and this Beale weren't involved in some antic and you weren't with Seaton's bunch, were you?'

'No!' said Calland indignantly. 'Would I have told you everything if I had anything to hide? It all happened just as I told you.'

'Yes, I guess it did,' said the marshal. 'Sorry I doubted you but a man's bound to be extra cautious when the Seaton bunch is in the vicinity. And you say this guy you met was named Beale?'

'Yes. Beale.'

'Beale,' repeated Riggs, frowning and pursing his lips. He seemed to fall into a moment or two of deep thought then he became enlivened, striding for the street door with Calland following. 'We'll call on Sim Jones at the telegraph office first,' he said.

The telegraph office was halfway along a set of stores on the town's only street and Sim Jones was a lean, elderly man with a shock of white hair and glasses balanced on the end of a bony nose. Bill Riggs introduced Calland to him and the telegrapher greeted the newcomer warmly.

'Pleased to see the arm of the law strengthened with the Jay Seaton gang not too far away,' he commented.

'The chief reason for our visit is the Seaton gang,' said Marshal Riggs. 'Is there any word on the telegraph wire about them?'

'The telegrapher in Stone Creek City sent a short message this morning. It seems they've cleared out of that region completely. The suspicion is they've probably bolted into Mexico to lie low for a spell.'

'Almost certainly,' said the marshal, 'but they'll be back on this side of the border before long for sure. In the gold camps there'll be nothing to steal but raw pay-dirt not yet turned into money. Banks are their real business and I'm wary of them hitting our bank.'

'You're right, Marshal. They've kept out of this country so far, but in other parts of the border they emptied a lot of bank vaults,' the telegrapher said. 'I'll have my Winchester close to hand just in case they show up.'

'Good thinking, Sim. I don't want to spread panic, but I'll warn every storekeeper and everyone on the street to have their firearms handy,' the marshal stated. 'Frank and I will stop off at the bank to warn the staff to be armed and ready for trouble. At the same time, everyone needs to keep a cool head and not go shooting unless there's real call for it.'

Sim Jones chuckled. 'Sounds like you're remembering the welcome those townsfolk up in Wyoming gave the Prothero brothers and their gang when they came looking for easy pickings. The whole darned town turned out, shooting and settling the hash of the Prothero crew for good and all.'

'You've got it right, Sim. But I was thinking what Wyoming can do well Arizona can do better.'

Marshal and deputy continued their tour of the street with Bill Riggs introducing Calland to the mayor, Amos Cotton, a powerfully built man with land interests in the region, who readily approved Riggs's choice of deputy. They met Art Givens, manager of the bank and his staff; the various storekeepers; Doc Chivers, the town's aged medico; Abe Scattergood, the lawyer; Ted Hawkes, the blacksmith and other notables. In every case, Bill Riggs warned of the need to be alert to the possibility of the Seaton gang arriving with their customary hurricane speed and to have firearms ready.

All the people to whom the new deputy was introduced struck him as typical of the settlers who came into the Southwest in this post-Civil War period. Santa Carmelita's citizens appeared to be solidly intent on settling down in new country and building new futures, after the wholesale disruption of the War.

It was known that some had fought for the North and some for the South but old wartime loyalties never came between neighbours in Santa Carmelita. Creating a wholesome community was the first of their aims in this year of 1873. Calland's overall impression of those he met was of a group he would be proud to serve with satisfaction.

One, however, irked the sensitivities that had been honed within him during his years as a young soldier and as a deputy law officer in the tumultuous Indian Territory. This was Tobias Terrell, the young partner of the lawyer, Abe Scattergood.

He was Scattergood's nephew, only recently qual-ified in law from a Boston college. He cut a languid figure in a sharp city suit and with much of the dandy about him. Leaning against a desk in Scattergood's office, smoking a cigar, he plainly did not think it worth his while to cease lounging and stand up as Calland was introduced to him.

He shook the deputy's hand while his look sug-gested he was offering a studied insult.

He had a smooth, not wholly trustworthy face and he made no conversation while Riggs and his deputy were in the office.

When they had departed, Abe Scattergood said: 'Our new deputy seems to be a smart young man. I figure he'll turn out to be the right one for the post or Marshal Riggs would never have sworn him in. Riggs is a rare judge of men.'

'Huh!' Terrell grunted. 'I'll tell you what I think of Riggs and his deputy—I'd say both of them are scared.'

'Riggs, scared!' echoed the lawyer. 'You haven't been in town long enough to know him. Everyone here will tell you he's been known to fight stacked odds—just himself and a six shooter and they've seen him do it right out there on that street.'

Terrell was unmoved. 'Look at the way they're

running around town, getting everyone ready to do their fighting for them if the Seaton gang shows up. They can make a brave sight, strutting around town with their tin stars, but when the chips are down, they expect others to do their job.'

'That's a grotesque notion, Tobe,' objected Scattergood. 'I'd back Riggs against anyone and his deputy looks like a fighting man. The precautions they suggest are plain common sense when you consider how the Seatons swoop into a town that's totally unready.'

'Sure, and you don't seem to realize that our noble marshal could be on the side of the Seaton gang. Just look at the way the country is going. Things are becoming unravelled in Washington,' stated Terrell. 'President Grant kept a tight grip on the South after the War, following the example of President Johnson before him and the Washington government handled the reconstruction of the South with an iron hand.

'But, in the last couple of years, Grant's become slack. The old rebel crew has managed to slowly work its way back into politics and has taken over in the Southern states. Before we know it, they'll start the War all over again. I shouldn't be surprised if they even re-established slavery.

'And they have sympathizers elsewhere, possibly right here in Santa Carmelita. In fact, I'm sure I heard something of the South in Riggs's accent.'

Abe Scattergood shook his head despairingly as his nephew unfolded his overblown theories.

'Take the Seaton bunch,' went on Terrill. 'Seaton was a rebel raider, equal to those bloodthirsty killers, Quantrill, Todd and Anderson, but he was never caught, shot or hanged. Maybe all the money he's collecting from banks is going to rebuild a warlike South. You must have heard that there are thousands down South who hanker to carry on the War, what with the Ku Klux Klan's raids on struggling folks and the interests of the Washington government and much more similar treasonable devilment.'

Terrell paused, took a breath and launched himself afresh into this subject with venomous enthusiasm. Plainly, he had a bee in his bonnet previously unknown to his uncle.

'I know President Grant claimed he wiped out the Klan with his act a couple of years ago, but everyone knows they merely went underground. Could be Marshal Riggs is secretly pro-South, as I'm sure many Southerners right here in southern Arizona are. Maybe he'd happily see Seaton's gang arrive in town and hit the bank. His new deputy, who is totally unknown to us, might also be happy. Riggs knows that these fat townsfolk are all enthusiasm for battle before the event but they'll be plain yellow in the face of a bloodthirsty outfit like the Seatons.'

Abe Scattergood gaped at his nephew. He was

seeing a side to him he never knew existed. Terrell sounded like a totally bigoted anti-Southerner, even a mentally unbalanced one, who could build up a wildly illogical fantasy of a scare story without anything like a shred of evidence.

'Maybe you were too long in Boston, absorbing those buttoned-up, puritanical principles of the folks up there, Tobe,' said Scattergood disgustedly. 'And, if you value your hide, don't call Bill Riggs a coward to his face. I don't know who he fought for in the war or even if he fought at all, nor does anyone else in town. There are neighbours here who fought on both sides but they buried the hatchet and came out here to start afresh.'

Much later that day, the lawyer had time to think about the twisted aspect of the mind of Tobe Terrell, the son of his sister, Rosina. After some reflection, he began to understand the root of it, though he remained disturbed by the intensity of his nephew's anti-Southern feeling.

Terrell's family were from Pennsylvania and comfortably off. His father, Joshua, was a lawyer, a profession traditionally followed by the Terrells. At the start of the War, when Abraham Lincoln sent out his call for a vast number of volunteers to fight the rebel South, Joshua responded early and was soon promoted to captain in a Pennsylvania volunteer infantry regiment. He distinguished himself in numerous early engagements until the brutal and bloody battle of Antietam in which he was killed.

Reports spoke of Captain Terrell putting up a spirited fight as usual but he fell in a savage bayonet attack by the Confederates. The lurid reports of Joshua's death affected the young Tobias Terrell deeply and he missed his good natured, fun-loving father. He formed an animosity towards the Southerners which did not diminish with the years but rather intensified into the unreasonable hatred which so shocked his uncle.

Abe Scattergood was conscious of the calumnies alleging devious and villainous dealings commonly hurled at lawyers in Western communities but he was a straight dealing and honest man. He sighed and hoped he would one day persuade his nephew to rid himself of his blind bigotry and see that all men, even Southerners, deserved to be honestly understood.

CHAPTER FOUR

A SHOT AT THE MARSHAL

After meeting several more citizens, introducing his new deputy and issuing warnings about the need to be armed and ready for the possible arrival of the Jay Seaton gang, Bill Riggs handed Calland the keys to the office which they had locked on starting their tour.

'I'm stepping over to Jack Grover's place. He's our gunsmith and he's straightening out a fault in a Colt of mine,' he said. 'Then I want to look in on Stanton's store, which is also our post office. I figure some wanted flyers will have been delivered by mail.

'Open up the office and you'll find the makings of coffee there. Boil up some coffee and we'll drink it as we go through the flyers and find out who among the wanted gentry might be drifting this way—in addition to Jay Seaton's crew, that is.'

On his return to the office, Calland was preparing coffee with his back to the street door when he heard a footstep. He turned to see a figure in the doorway, the trim figure of a girl in a neat shirtwaist and a long, full skirt which gave her a fashion-plate appearance imparting an up to the moment touch of chic rare in frontier women.

The bright sunlight of the street at her back emphasized her attractively coiffed hair, showing it to be of a glowing copper colour. She carried a large bundle, wrapped in a blanket.

Calland felt an unaccustomed lifting of his heart at the sight of the girl. With the sun behind her, she seemed to be a youthful, almost mythical creation of the light.

As she moved out of the sun's brassy glare in the doorway and into the shade of the office, her face became more defined. She had a fresh beauty, a classically formed face and wide, hazel eyes.

The eyes considered Calland with a steady, almost calculating look, not exactly hostile but suggesting a certain caution. Maybe, thought Calland, she did not like men.

She dumped the bundle on the floor and said, 'Dad sent me with some fresh bedding. The bed in your room has not been properly made up since that fellow Harry Schultz departed.'

'Dad?' asked Calland.

'Yes, my father—Marshal Riggs,' she said. 'Maybe he didn't tell you he has a daughter. I guess he was just too tied up in giving you all the details of the marshalling job, which'd be typical of him. I'm Rosemary Riggs.' She did not offer her hand and her eyes suggested she was still measuring him up.

'And I'm Frank Calland.'

'Yes, I know. Dad told me about you. He called in on his way to the gunsmith's a few minutes ago and asked me to bring this bundle to the office. We have a small house a little way along the street. My mother died four years ago and I keep house for my father.'

She nodded to the bundle on the floor.

'I'll leave this with you and bid you good day,' she said and turned for the door.

Calland watched her step out into the street where the bright sunlight seemed to contrast with her demeanour. Was she as aloof and frosty as she seemed or merely of a detached, business-like temperament? A strange girl, he thought, whose not-quite-belligerent attitude contrasted so strongly with her perfectly moulded classical features and her fine hazel eyes.

He recalled that there was more than a hint of unfriendliness in her tone when she had referred to 'that fellow Harry Schultz'. Did she have a down on all men or just on his predecessor Schultz? Perhaps, for some reason, she reserved a special dislike for all young deputy marshals. He found that a thoroughly gloomy thought.

He took the bundle of bedding and dumped it on

his bed and he had concluded preparing the coffee when Marshal Riggs returned, carrying the latest batch of wanted flyers, collected from the post office.

'I just had a visit from your daughter,' said Calland.

'Oh, so you met Rosemary. I guess I never had a chance to tell you about her,' said Riggs. 'She's a gem of a girl and a huge help to me but I'll admit I often have a troubled conscience about her.'

'Why should you have?'

'Well, she had her heart set on going off to college to take up school teaching. I know she has brains enough to make a success of it and have a good career for herself. But when my wife died, she figured it was her duty to stay at home and back me up in my job. She didn't feel it right to leave me to cope with the town marshal's job and take care of myself at the same time.

'I tried to persuade her to go for the career she wanted, but she wouldn't listen to me. Nothing could make her do anything but what she saw as her duty. I'm always grateful for such a caring daughter … but sometimes I think I'm depriving her of something very important to her.'

Calland recalled the girl's cold attitude which he had perhaps misunderstood for animosity towards males. Maybe relinquishing the path in life she had desired to follow had left some bitterness in her, although he was sure she was devoted to her father.

He tried to look at things from her point of view.

She would certainly understand that Bill Riggs's stead-fast devotion to his post could lead to his violent death on Santa Carmelita's dusty street any day and she had no doubt inherited his same devotion to what she saw as a plain duty, so she stood by her father.

Over coffee, he and Riggs considered the newest wanted flyers, a set of reward posters for various men active in recent criminal activities in New Mexico and Arizona, and at various points along the border between Arizona and the Mexican state of Sonora.

One of the very latest was devoted to the bank robbery in Stone Creek City by the Jay Seaton gang. It was embellished by crude line engravings purporting to show the faces of the perpetrators of the crime. The names of all the gang were known and each portrait bore a name.

Calland considered the drawings closely, stabbed one with his finger and drew Bill Riggs's attention to it.

'This one's described as Beale, the name of the joker I met on the desert, and it says here he is some-times known as Daggett,' he said. 'But the drawing is so poor he could be anybody.'

Riggs took the poster from him and scrutinized it closely. Calland recalled how he had appeared to be particularly interested in the name of Beale when he mentioned it on first meeting the marshal. After his lengthy study of the portrait, the marshal went on to read the details of Seaton's latest outrage, the bank raid in Stone Creek City with its lurid account of the fatal shooting of the teller, Seth Cooper, a young father of two children.

'You say you heard someone yell something about this murder when this Beale and you were in Stone Creek City?' queried Riggs. 'He pointed to Beale, but did he say Beale did the killing?'

'Not so far as I remember. He just shouted that Beale was a member of the Seaton gang on the raid in which the teller was killed.'

Marshal Riggs looked again at the portrait bearing Beale's name, giving it intense scrutiny. Only this man among the whole set of Seaton's gang of raiders illustrated seemed to have a peculiar fascination for him.

'This crew have a fair tally of murder counts against them,' he said at length. 'If they're convicted, they're the kind who're likely to be hanged in bulk, including those who were not individually responsible for murder.

'It says here they are believed to be over the border in Mexico. They'll never find rich pickings over there so they'll come back into the US pretty soon for sure. They could show up anywhere along the border. Maybe here in Arizona or maybe New Mexico or Texas but I'm going to make sure this town gives 'em all hell if they show their noses here.'

Over the border in Mexico, a conference was in progress. In the gloomy room in the old house, the

Seaton gang stood around paying attention to Jay Seaton who was sprawling on the old couch like some languid emperor, but there was nothing languid in his delivery of conjectured plans.

Even his naturally slow Southern drawl was replaced by a rapid pronunciation when he spoke of gaining money through lightning bank raids. It was a subject about which his crew of plunderers were always happy to hear.

Normally, the Seaton gang worked to a schedule that had proved successful. They would make perhaps two or three bank raids on towns spaced from each other by some distance, then go to ground for a spell.

Each member would carry his share of hard cash off to his own personal bolt-hole in some far distant state or territory. There, many lived outwardly respectable lives on the proceeds of their raiding.

After a time, usually when there were rumours of some region over the wide map of the frontier enjoying tempting bonanza times, Jay Seaton would send out the call to gather at some convenient rendezvous, perhaps even in the anonymity of some large city, to draw up a plan of campaign. Thus, another season of speedy raids out West would open.

Seaton was always careful to be sure his men were well scattered when not raiding so they could never be pinpointed and their robberies were spread over such a vast extent of territory it was impossible for the authorities to guess where they would strike next.

His raiders had perpetrated a spate of town burnings, robberies and brutal murders in the conflict between the states. They had never been 'reconstructed' in the post-war attempts to re-make the Union into one body and had no intention of buckling down to peace time life.

Jay Seaton, however, used his brains in his approach to his lawless business. He knew that the haphazard ways of the wartime bands were no longer suited to an era when the forces of law were becoming more sophisticated and widespread. Big scale robbery required a general's strategy.

His strategy was balanced and he took care that one raid was not staged too soon after another and that the target bank was not in a town geographically close to the one just raided.

He had, however, acquired some tempting information about Santa Carmelita.

Although that town was not far from Stone Creek City, where the gang had so recently grabbed a fat haul of loot, he was of a mind to break his own rule and raid its bank fairly soon.

Seaton believed in complete unity of purpose among the crew, and wanted no half-heartedness that could lead to a venture being botched or even wrecked. He called this gathering to plumb the general feeling about leaving the safety of Mexico to cross the border with Santa Carmelita as the target.

His men made a motley gathering in their trail-punished clothing, intimidating side arms and their array of shaggy beards and moustaches with a cloud of tobacco smoke from cigars, pipes and cigarillos hovering over their heads.

They heard Seaton outline his plan, conferred with each other and declared themselves in full agreement with it. The prospect of soon adding a cut of further loot to that from the Stone Creek City venture lured every man away from the usual pattern of caution.

'Very well,' said Seaton. 'I've heard rumours about Santa Carmelita. Even though I don't know as much as I want to know, I heard the town is probably ripe for our attention. There's one big ranch in the locality, the Box BS, and a few smaller ones. On the whole, it is thriving on the beef business, what with contracts to feed the army and government contracts for the Indian reservations. There are a good number of businesses in town, too. It adds up to a heap of money making its one and only bank good and fat.' He paused and fixed his eyes on Cal Daggett. 'When the time comes for us to say adios to Mexico, we'll keep a date with that bank, so get ready to do your usual spying stuff, Daggett. We'll follow the trusted old pattern and not make a move until we have all the information we need.'

'Me? Why is it always me?' protested Daggett.

'Because you've proved you're good at it, though it

pains me to give you any praise,' said Seaton harshly. 'You're hardly worth a damned thing, but you're good at spying out everything a well-organized outfit like ours needs to know before it goes into action. You're neither handsome nor ugly. You have the kind of face that folks forget which is useful when you snoop around a strange town.' His voice dropped to a low and sinister level as he added, 'And you brought the whole damned bunch of us one step closer to the hangman's rope when you shot that teller in Stone Creek City. You need to redeem yourself, Daggett.'

Daggett looked resentful but there was no way of arguing with Seaton and the rest of the gang who were enthusiastic about netting another profitable haul of plunder. To a man, they glowered at him, communicating the unspoken message to quit squawking and do as Seaton ordered.

Daggett saw he had no choice. He had lost face with his outlaw colleagues and the only way he could regain their trust was to comply with Seaton's orders and, once again, take on the role of spy and assess the Santa Carmelita bank as the target for a projected raid.

The day after the conference, he was shaven and spruced up to look like some respectable horseback traveller. His holstered Colt was worn belted too high at the waist, suggesting he was not in the habit of going armed and did so only because of the dangers he might meet on the trail. Riding low at his thigh, as it usually was, would betray him as one accustomed to using the weapon.

He rode an ill-defined desert trail in an apprehensive mood. He had no great enthusiasm for the task Jay Seaton had ordered him to undertake. The trail led over a sweltering landscape whose barren, rock-studded vistas were occasionally broken by clumps of green saguaro cactus and Joshua trees. Eventually, this trail widened out and transformed itself into the main street of Santa Carmelita.

In the town, Daggett had to investigate those important points Seaton was insistent on knowing before mounting a lightning strike on the bank. At the same time, Daggett needed to keep up a front as a bland-faced anonymous stranger. He had played the role before and had to acknowledge the truth of Seaton's observation that he had the kind of face people quickly forgot. His previous forays into pre-raid spying had always proved successful. Not once had a citizen ever become suspicious of his motives or challenged him.

But he had nagging doubts about the current venture. He could not explain it but, from the start, he was haunted by the notion that something would go wrong.

Such was his apprehension that he almost turned back as the outlines of the town appeared beyond a shimmering heat haze. But he knew he could not back out of the work to which Jay Seaton had forced him to set his hand. The avaricious ambitions of a set of dangerous hard cases rode on a successful raid on the Santa Carmelita bank and Cal Daggett was essential to the unfolding of their plan.

Cal Daggett had everything timed to a nicety. He entered the town on almost the stroke of noon, an hour when a large portion of the populace who had no particular business on hand retired for a siesta. The mounting torpor of midday gripped the street.

He rode into a street nearly empty of humanity. No horses were tethered at the hitch racks. There were two or three wagons drawn up against the plank walks, their horses looking sleepy between the shafts and switching at the flies with their tails in an equally sleepy manner.

With narrowed eyes, Daggett tried to take in as much of both sides of the street as he could survey in spite of the glare of the sun. He saw store fronts, a couple of saloons, structures bearing the titles of doctor and attorney and one which immediately engaged his attention bore a shingle labelled *Town Marshal* and, in brackets beneath that title *William Riggs*.

It was disconcerting to note that this office was immediately opposite the solid frame structure of the Santa Carmelita bank, but what caused both Daggett's mouth and eyes to open wide was the name of the marshal lettered on the shingle. He stared hard at it for a moment, seeming to have been hypnotized.

'My God ... Bill Riggs!' he breathed. Then, as if sight of the name spurred him to recollecting that he had a task to perform, he came to life and began to act quickly and purposefully.

There was no sign of life around the vicinity of the bank which had four hitch rails outside its gallery. It was safe to assume that customers at the bank were few at this hour. With half an eye on the frontage of the marshal's office, Daggett pulled rein at the bank, dismounted, tied up his mount at a hitch rack, walked up the four plank steps to the gallery and entered. The interior was empty of customers and Daggett put his powers of observation into swift action, mentally noting details of the interior.

There was a long counter with four tellers working on it and it was without any wire frame or barrier between customer and teller, which meant any raider might easily jump over it. He noted the exact position of the big iron safe at the back of the counter; the positioning of doors, doubtless to inner offices and he paid particular attention to one marked *Manager.* It was from there that, in the progress of a raid, the bank official most responsible for guarding the bank's riches might emerge, possibly armed.

Cal Daggett quickly had the whole lay-out imprinted on his mind so that he could draw an accurate sketch map if needed and he halted close to the nearest teller, a skinny, elderly man with glasses balanced on the end of his nose. Daggett had primed himself with a line of conversation which included the name of a small town some distance away, Silica Wells.

'I'm a stranger in these parts and on my way to Silica Wells,' he told the teller. 'I just called in to ask if anyone might know where an old friend named Horace Arbuthnot lives. I was told some years ago that he had settled somewhere around Santa Carmelita.' He had manufactured the name of Horace Arbuthnot, knowing that it was unlikely there was anyone of that name in all Arizona.

The elderly teller scratched his head. 'No, sir,' he said. 'I can't recollect anyone of that name living in town or anywhere around here and I've been here for a good many years.' He called along the counter to the next man:

'Hey, Fred, ever know of a man named Horace Arbuthnot somewhere in these parts?'

The neighbouring teller looked blank. 'No. He ain't one of our customers, for sure,' he responded.

Daggett shrugged. 'I guess I was misinformed,' he said.

Two minutes later, he was back at the hitch rail, loosening his rein. He freed his horse and swung into the saddle and at that very moment, saw a stolid figure striding across the street from the marshal's office. He wore a lawman's star on his buckskin vest and he stopped for an instant and stared at Daggett as if he could not believe his eyes, then he quickened his pace towards the mounted man.

Daggett's mouth and eyes became wide open at the same time. For a moment, he appeared to be totally paralysed, staring at Riggs unbelievingly. A gasping sound escaped him and he managed to splutter, 'My God! Bill! Of all people—Bill!"

Like a man possessed, he whirled his horse around, spurred it savagely, sending it at top speed off along the street in the direction from which he had entered while Marshal Bill Riggs called after him urgently, 'Hey—hold hard!'

Daggett had put a back trail clouded by swirling dust between himself and the lawman and he turned with a Colt revolver in his hand. He blasted a hasty, wild shot back at Riggs and it screamed past his head, well off target.

Inside the marshal's office, Frank Calland heard the shot and rushed out into the street. He saw a straggle of people coming out of various premises, including several employees spilling down the steps of the bank. Marshal Bill Riggs was lying on his back in the rutted dust of the street. Calland had the immediate impression that he had been killed.

He ran to the marshal, only dimly aware that others were converging on the still form, hastening from the bank and various nearby buildings. He was aware, too, that a horseman was speeding off behind a cloud of hoof-stirred dust. He looked at the fast dwindling animal and rider and, just as he did so, the man in the saddle turned his head and looked back.

Shock jolted through Calland as, in spite of the swirls of dust and the distance of the rider, he could fleetingly see something of the man's face and he had the impression that he seemed to look like the man he met on the desert—the man he knew as Beale.

He automatically grabbed at his holstered Colt, prodded by the instinct to ride after him. Then he remembered that his horse, with that of Bill Riggs, was tethered in the yard behind the marshal's office. With mounting anxiety, he looked around for an animal somewhere on the street but saw none at the nearest hitch racks. Then his concern for the welfare of the marshal made him concentrate on running towards him.

Just as he reached Riggs, he suddenly saw that Rosemary was there, seeming to have materialized out of the blue. She was bending over the still form of her father with an agonized expression and beginning to cradle his head in her arms. His eyes were closed and he was motionless. Calland was sure Bill Riggs, a lawman with sharp intelligence and a noted savvy of the perils of his calling, had been killed in a foggily obscure incident virtually on the doorstep of his office.

'Dad!' gasped Rosemary, half choking. 'Dad—where are you hit?'

Riggs shuddered. His eyes opened and he looked around like a man emerging from a deep slumber. He pushed himself up on his elbows and looked at the concerned citizens crowding around him, then shook himself free from his daughter's embrace, grasped her hand and squeezed it.

'I'm all right,' he said. 'I wasn't hit. For some reason, that joker took it into his head to shoot at me. I was ducking his bullet and I guess I stumbled and hit my head.'

Calland and Rosemary helped him to his feet. Calland stared at him in bewilderment. There was something illogical about the whole incident. He saw nothing of it but heard the shot then saw Riggs lying on his back.

From what he heard of Riggs, he had pictured a man with such a dynamic reputation that if he saw the mounted man go for his gun, he would have cleared his holster leather with lightning speed and blasted an effective shot at him. Instead there was this limp anti-climax of his stumbling and somehow losing consciousness while the rider split the wind to get out of town.

Surely, when a man stumbled he fell forward and not onto his back. It sounded like a contrived and lame excuse.

Then there was the matter of the face of the departing horseman. Calland was almost certain he was Beale. He had an imperative urge to catch up with the man, coupled with an acute sense of failure and shame. Before an audience of townsfolk, he and the marshal looked as if they had been caught flat-footed and must appear utterly inept in the eyes of the citizens who entrusted them with enforcing the law.

But there was still no horse immediately to hand.

'Marshal—that man must be caught,' he spluttered indignantly. 'He had a reason for shooting at you. I'm getting a horse and going after him and—' Bill Riggs cut him off in mid-sentence with a restraining hand on his arm.

'Forget it, Frank,' he said. 'He'll be far away by now or he's probably hidden himself away in the desert.'

Calland stared at him, not wholly believing what he was hearing. It looked as if the marshal did not want the departed rider to be pursued.

Now, further doubts concerning this incident began to fortify the initial ones. He recalled that, when they were studying the wanted flyers and the name of Beale, sometimes called Daggett, came up among the members of the Seaton gang, Riggs had shown an interest in him. More than once he made reference to him and the crude drawing which was supposed to depict him. Could it be that he knew Beale or was in some way connected to him?

Was that why Riggs was so pointedly reluctant to pursue him?

*

The lawyer Tobe Terrell was standing at the upstairs window of his uncle's attorney's office almost over-looking the spot where the drama involving the marshal was played out. He was alone in the room and had been looking out onto the street for some time. He saw the whole affair unwind.

He witnessed the unknown stranger emerge from the bank, right across the street. He saw Marshal Riggs approach him from his own office on the same side of the street as the lawyer's premises. He could not hear any conversation but watched the incident performed in dumb-play.

He saw Bill Riggs stop near the stranger just as he straddled his horse and speak to him. The stranger stared at the lawman, made some remark then hastily turned his mount, spurred it and galloped away. Then he turned with a drawn pistol and fired at Riggs.

There then occurred the most astonishing aspect of the whole drama. The shot went well wide of Riggs and Terrell saw the bullet kick up a spurt of dust in the street a long way behind Riggs. Beyond doubt, Riggs was unscathed yet the marshal fell backwards and lay still as if shot.

Terrell reflected on this fact as he absently watched the marshal being helped to his feet by his daughter and his deputy.

The dandified northerner had taken up his uncle's

offer of a partnership in his frontier practice, though he viewed the populace of Arizona with suspicion and contempt due to his unbridled animosity towards the culture of the Old South.

From its earliest history as a territory of the United States, Arizona hosted a great many Southern adventurers. Early in the Civil War, there was even an attempt to make a Confederate territory of the region, soon scotched by Union troops. Now, nearly a decade after the War, the South still had diehard elements reacting violently against its 'reconstruction' by the North.

The lawyer saw treason everywhere and he felt that, even here in Arizona, dangerous pro-Southern plots were being hatched.

Tobe Terrell's twisted bias gave him a wholesale suspicion of Arizona folk. He saw Bill Riggs and his deputy urging the townsfolk to resist any raid by the Seaton gang as a move to get others to do the fighting that was the sworn duty of officers of the law. But it was mere window-dressing because the townsfolk would be overwhelmed by the ferocity of a crew of killers led by a former Confederate guerrilla chieftain.

The bank raid would take place and the takings would go towards revitalizing a new rebel South.

Terrell tried to recall the face of the man who fired at Riggs but found he could not. It was a totally bland face, unremarkable in every way—a very forgettable face.

There must certainly be something between this anonymous-faced man and Riggs, so often characterized as a dogged, bullet-spitting lawman, but who let the horseman ride away then performed a spurious charade when he was fired on.

The devious and suspicious mind of Tobe Terrell began to work overtime on yet more fantasies with the South cast as villain. It was an attitude of mind which threw his relationship with the people of Santa Carmelita out of kilter. For, in truth, to a man, the citizenry strove to overcome old enmities and build new futures after the bloodthirsty cataclysm of the great Civil War.

CHAPTER FIVE

MENACE ON THE DESERT

'I'm quite all right. There's no need to fuss,' insisted Marshal Bill Riggs. 'I simply stumbled, that's all. I'm not hurt in any way.'

He was seated in a chair in the marshal's office into which his daughter and deputy had planted him on bringing him in from the street. Rosemary stood beside him, deeply concerned, with a hand on his shoulder.

'Are you sure you're not hurt, Dad? I was coming out of the store after shopping when I saw you and the stranger on the horse just before he moved off so fast. Then he turned and shot at you,' said Rosemary. 'When you fell over it looked as if he had hit you. You seemed to talk to him before it happened.'

'I did. It was merely a matter of passing the time of day with a stranger. Anyone policing a town as near to the border as this one does well to notice strangers and there's no harm in letting them know they've been noticed.'

'And you didn't know him?' asked Calland cautiously.

'Not from Adam but I aim to find out something about him,' Riggs said. 'He came out of the bank and someone over there might know why he visited the bank. I'll step over there in a few minutes and ask a few questions. You go on home, Rosemary, and quit worrying about me. I'll be with you for supper. We must ask Frank along for a meal one day, if he'd care to join us.'

'I'd be happy to. Thanks for the invitation,' said Calland.

Rosemary's father assured her once more that he was perfectly fit, then she gave Calland a nod in which there was only slight cordiality and left.

The incident involving the stranger in town continued to irk Calland as, from the office door, he watched the marshal walk across the street to the bank. He could not rid his mind of the notion that Bill Riggs knew the rider who looked like the outlaw named either Beale or Daggett.

Marshal Riggs spent about ten minutes at the bank and returned, frowning.

'The stranger never gave any name. He just called in to ask if anyone knew the whereabouts of a man supposed to live somewhere in this vicinity, a man no one ever heard of,' he reported to Calland. 'It's plenty suspicious. In all the time the Seaton gang have been operating along the frontier, there have been yarns claiming that their way of working inside a bank they've raided suggests familiarity with its layout. They always know exactly where the principal safe is and where the tellers are located in relation to the doors for a speedy strike then a quick exit. It all points to someone having scouted the place beforehand. Probably, they send a man in with some phony inquiry before the raid.'

'Ah,' breathed Calland, 'that's why you were suspicious of the joker who shot at you. You knew he was a stranger and wondered why he had called in at the bank.'

'Sure, I've been on the alert ever since word got out that the Seatons are in the border country. I spotted him as he came out of the bank and he seemed to look like one of the men on the wanted flyers.

'The story that the Seatons sent in a man to do some advance scouting was on my mind so I figured I'd question him discreetly and saw no reason to pull my gun. That was a mistake. I never expected him to haze off and shoot back at me. Then I stumbled.

'I guess I made the whole of Santa Carmelita's law enforcement apparatus—that's you and me—look like damned fools in front of the whole town. I'm sorry about that that.'

Calland shrugged. He now felt less uneasy about his notion that Riggs and the stranger knew each other but there was still a query over the marshal's stumble, causing him to fall on his back. But what he had just heard alerted him to a more pressing matter.

'So, I guess you're pretty sure our visitor was spying out the bank's layout and we can expect Daggett's bunch to raid sooner or later,' he said. 'And I guess the stranger *was* Beale or Daggett or whatever he chooses to call himself.'

'I'm plumb sure of it now I know why he visited the bank,' replied Riggs. 'We don't know where the gang is right now—in Mexico or on this side of the border. Could be they're somewhere out on the desert, almost under our noses and ready to swoop at any moment. The only thing we can be certain about is that they'll be showing up—with our bank in their sights! I told the staff to expect danger and assured them that steps have been taken to have as many of the citizens as possible ready to fight off the Seatons as soon as they show up.'

A sense of urgency took over in the marshal's office with Riggs and Calland going through a programme of tasks aimed at preparedness and Calland saw that the marshal had a broad procedure to be put into place when danger threatened Santa Carmelita, whether from marauding outlaw bands or the still unsubdued tribes such as the Apaches or Yaquis.

The rack of a dozen Winchester rifles kept beside the door in case citizens needed to be sworn in as deputies if some extraordinary emergency arose were checked over. Their magazines were found to be full and their actions oiled and in working order. Cases of rifle and pistol ammunition were brought from the closet at the rear of the office room, normally kept firmly locked. They were opened and conveniently placed near the rifle rack in readiness to replenish weapons.

Bill Riggs drew a wooden inner shutter across half of the window facing the bank and ensured that the other half could be quickly opened to allow shots to be fired at the bank from inside the office.

From his desk drawer, the marshal took a sheet of paper and read out a list of townsmen who, long before, had made a standing commitment to take on the role of deputy marshal if ever there was an emergency.

On it were such notables as Dave Cox, of the eating house across the street and Sim Jones, the telegraphist who reserved the right to do his deputizing, keeping watch from within his office, knowing there might be need for Santa Carmelita to have a channel of communication to the outside world.

The gunsmith Jack Grover, a useful man to have in the midst of action involving gunplay, was also on the list.

With such men as these, plus the bulk of responsible citizenry already warned to be ready for a raid by the Seatons, Calland marvelled at how thoroughly Bill Riggs had laid down the defences of Santa Carmelita, starting even before there was any threat from the Seaton gang.

'Now all we have to do is visit our volunteer deputies, take them their badges and swear them in,' said Bill Riggs, on concluding the preparations in the office.

In Paso Jacinto, Mexico, a little earlier that evening, Jay Seaton was in conference with his scout, Cal Daggett. In his hand he had a paper bearing a rough sketch map of the interior of the Carmelita bank.

It gave accurate information as to the positioning of doors, the large safe and the locations where staff were likely to be working.

Seaton had closely studied the map and had committed its salient points to memory.

'You say the safe is one of the old-style iron pattern, so that'll mean getting the keys from the chief teller or maybe from the boss of the bank unless we're lucky enough to hit the place when the safe is open,' he said. 'That could slow things down, particularly if whoever holds them is ornery and puts up some resistance. Getting into the safe will be essential because what we will get by making an over the counter grab will not be worth the effort.

'Four men must be detailed to go in with the first rush and concentrate on nothing but finding who has the keys, getting them and opening up the safe.' He paused, gave a mysterious chuckle and added, 'If that blamed safe is too stubborn, I have a neat trick up my sleeve that'll open it.'

He pointed to a small but dangerous object on the floor near his feet, a wooden gunpowder keg with a fuse trailing from it, an object easily acquired in San Jacinto where all manner of aids to mining operations were available.

'What's the word on the law in the town?'

'Not good,' said Daggett. 'The marshal's office is almost directly opposite the bank. It's only yards away.'

'Hell!' snorted Seaton.

'And the marshal is Bill Riggs. He has quite a reputation at that end of Arizona.'

'Blast it! His reputation is a damned sight wider than that. I never ran up against him but I heard plenty about him. I thought the place would have some half-asleep hick as marshal. I never figured on Riggs.'

'Neither did I,' said Daggett dispiritedly.

In fact, Daggett's spirits had been low ever since his face-to-face meeting with Marshal Bill Riggs, an encounter about which he was determined to say nothing to Jay Seaton. Under no circumstances would he ever reveal to the gang's chieftain or his followers that there was a close relationship between himself and the marshal of Santa Carmelita.

His heart was in his boots because of the planned raid and, if he could have deserted the gang, he would have taken to his heels. But there was no way of quitting Jay Seaton's outfit nor was there any way he could avoid participation in the bank raid. The best he could hope for was that, this time, his mask did not slip and his presence among the raiders went un-noticed by Marshal Bill Riggs, for he knew Riggs would certainly spearhead armed resistance to the raid.

'How many deputies does Riggs have?' asked Seaton.

'I don't know. I didn't have time to find out and there were no obvious deputies hanging around the front of the office.'

'So, how do you know Riggs is the marshal?'

'His name is on a shingle above the office door.'

Seaton scrutinized the sketch map again. 'We'll have to pay extra attention to that damned office. We'll have six men planted in front of the bank to deal with anyone on the street and, in particular, to handle any danger from the marshal's office.'

He looked at the map again for a further five minutes to verify various points then said,

'We move tomorrow. It's going to be hot so we'll start early and take our time on the trail so we don't arrive in town too tuckered out to do our stuff. And you, Daggett, watch your itchy trigger finger and don't bring the whole bunch of us any nearer the hangman's rope.'

Another night passed and an almost crushing anticipation of danger seemed to settle over the marshal's office with the dawning of a new day. More precisely it settled over Marshal Bill Riggs and Deputy Marshal Frank Calland because, since Riggs's visit to the bank, both were certain it had been singled out for the imminent brutal attentions of Jay Seaton and his robbers.

It was largely an acute sense of waiting which started that morning after the two law officers had sworn in the deputies. It had mounted since the previous night when the pair split the hours of darkness with Calland taking four hours of night duty around the office and patrolling the street, while Riggs took the next four until dawn, leaving his home for a lonesome, watchful turn. Both men found all quiet under the warm blanket of the desert night.

With the dawning, the warmth of the air became hot to add to the irksome heaviness of anticipation. It was as if nature had decided to shed the pleasant spring conditions and abruptly immerse Santa Carmelita in a burst of high summer before that season was due.

Flies and other unwanted insects buzzed in through the open door and the perspiring lawmen swatted at them, mopped their brows and waited … and waited … and waited in an atmosphere of climbing tension.

Well before noon, Calland came in after patrolling the street and checking the wellbeing of the horses tied in the yard, then bringing them to be hitched at the racks in front of the office. A notion smote him during his patrolling and he decided to put it before

Bill Riggs, who was sitting behind his desk, fanning himself with his hat.

'Yesterday, you said the Seatons might be out in the desert, maybe even under our noses, getting ready to swoop on the town but we haven't any idea where they are. Maybe they haven't even left Mexico,' said Calland. 'I'm getting almighty tired of sweating it out and just waiting. How would it be if I rode out yonder to take a look around to see if there's any sign of them?"

'Hell no, that'd be too dangerous!' exploded Riggs. 'A lone man going up against that crew would be asking for trouble. The whole bunch would be down on your neck as soon as they spotted you.'

Calland gave a wry smile. 'Who says they'll spot me? I fought the Apaches with the army, remember. I learned a thing or two about desert warfare from running up against Yellow Hoof's braves. They could suddenly appear before you from being damned near invisible and we had to learn fast.'

Riggs rubbed his chin and thought for a while. 'Well, it would be more than useful to know if the Seatons are within striking distance. It might ease the waiting in this infernal heat to have some solid information. Go ahead, but don't cook your goose by meeting up with them face-to-face on the trail.'

'No danger of that. The Navajo scouts with my army outfit were pretty good instructors. I could start right now. My horse is fresh and newly watered. I need only the barest of rations and a full canteen of water—oh, and a good strong blanket, brown or grey with no pattern. One of those Rosemary brought would be just right.'

'Well, I have every faith in the desert savvy you learned in the cavalry, but take care you don't put a foot wrong,' cautioned Riggs, standing at the door of the office as Calland packed some hard rations into the saddle bag on his horse.

Sparsely equipped with only the essentials for travelling over the desert, Calland set off at a smart pace but once out of town and on the desert trail, he eased the pace to spare his bronc early fatigue.

He travelled Apache fashion, coming off the well trafficked main trail into town and riding the ridges beside it. With their humps of land, clusters of boulders and stands of cactus and Joshua trees, they offered immediate cover if it was needed as well as a high vantage point over the trail. The sun neared its noon zenith and blazed out of a clean azure sky, putting a wavering heat haze on the far line of hills beyond which lay Mexico. Those hills were his main point of reference.

So long as he could see them, even when the trail was obscured from view, he knew he was heading south and the hypnotic trickery of the sweltering desert had not enticed him off course.

It was a sweaty and weary wayfaring in which

Calland allowed his horse to take its own pace over the uncertain terrain of the ridge, running parallel to the trail out of Mexico. Whenever he looked down on the trail from the shelter of boulders of clumps of tall saguaro cactus, it proved to be empty of traffic travelling one way or the other. He began to wonder if Jay Seaton was not ready to mount a raid. True, he had sent in a spy to test the potential of the Santa Carmelita bank but was that proof that a raid was planned imminently?

Possibly, Seaton would hold off for some days and perhaps for even longer. After all, the gang had only recently grabbed a presumably profitable haul at Stone Creek City.

While his thoughts were running along such lines, Calland spotted a couple of black shapes in the sky. He halted his horse, narrowed his eyes against the oppressive glare of the sun and stared at them. He saw that they were birds, flapping big wings and making languid circles against the bright blue of the sky.

'Turkey buzzards!' he muttered to his bronc. 'They're a sure sign of life—or, maybe, death!'

He touched spurs to his mount's hide and continued his steady ride onward, keeping an eye on the sky. As if from nowhere, another pair of winged dots joined the circling birds.

'Something plumb interesting is attracting those critters,' he murmured to himself. 'Maybe it's a dead animal on the trail or maybe a dead man—or maybe just men who're alive and kicking and fixing grub. Those damned buzzards will swoop down on any scraps or anything else that's eatable.'

Nearly half an hour later, his heart quickened when he saw a blur of grey smoke directly under the point where the turkey buzzards were flying. He pushed on a little further then he spotted movement down at the trail side below the ridge.

There was a stand of thin timber there and clusters of tall, crooked-armed saguaro cactus, certain signs of a waterhole.

Halting his mount in the lee of some large, sun-split rocks, he swung down from the saddle, took his heavy grey blanket from his saddlebag, wrapped it around himself, even covering his head, lay on the ground then crawled, Indian fashion to the very edge of the ridge where he lay among scattered rocks.

He had a vantage point from which, by keeping a corner of the blanket lifted, he could see the waterhole below. He knew that the covering blanket made him appear to be just another rock along the rock-studded edge of the ridge.

There were horses lined up at the waterhole. He counted fourteen. There were over a dozen men visible, some tending a cooking fire from which smoke drifted up while others sat around eating or smoking. All had the look of frontier hard cases. They were too far away for faces to be distinguished but Calland felt the man he first knew as Beale was among them.

So, Jay Seaton and his gang were en route to Santa Carmelita and he had their strength—at least fourteen, and all looked to be heavily armed. They were taking their time and had stopped for water and to cook up some grub. Probably, after this respite, they would put on some speed and could possibly strike Santa Carmelita about mid-afternoon, a time when desert townships frequently took a siesta.

Calland's thoughts now turned to the urgency of returning to Santa Carmelita with the news that the Seatons were on the way.

He was about to slither down the rear of the ridge to where he had left his bronc when he saw one of the men squatting beside the waterhole stand up and walk across the trail, heading for the rising land at the top of which Calland lay under the cover of his blanket. He walked slowly, watching the ground. He stopped once or twice and picked up some scraps of dried out wood, shed by some of the spindly, desert punished shrubbery that tried to flourish here and there along the slope of the ridge.

Calland watched from under the edge of the blanket and realized he was collecting fuel to feed the cooking fire the group had set at the edge of the waterhole. He began to walk up the ridge, still searching the ground and Calland was acutely aware that, if he came much closer, there was a danger he would notice one of the humps among the apparent rocks on the crest of the ridge was a blanket, concealing a watcher.

Calland slipped his hand down below his waist to grip the butt of his holstered Colt. He began to calculate his chances of getting away with a whole skin if he was discovered and the Seatons came after him and shooting started. He had the advantage of being on high ground while they were down beside the trail but scooting in retreat down the rocky rear of the ridge to reach his horse would not be easy.

The man, a paunchy individual with an unkempt beard who advertised his outlaw status by wearing a Mexican style ammunition band studded with rifle shells across his chest, came nearer, then a trifle nearer. Calland gritted his teeth and eased the Colt in its leather.

Then, with his arms almost filled with tinder, the Seaton outlaw turned, trudged down the ridge and began to cross the trail to join his fellows.

Calland breathed easier. He squinted at the men on the further side of the trail, ascertained that none were looking his way then, still keeping the blanket over him as cover, slithered back on his belly until he was below the rim of the ridge.

He gathered up the blanket, mounted the bronc and rode back toward Santa Carmelita at the rear of the ridge until well clear of the waterhole and the

Seatons, then took to the main trail and spurred his mount to a smarter pace.

He burst into the marshal's office where he found Marshal Bill Riggs leaning against his desk, examining the action of one of the newly introduced 1873 pattern Winchester rifles.

'They're on the way!' reported Calland. 'Fourteen of them. They were at the waterhole nearest town and I reckon maybe an hour and a half of steady riding will bring them here.'

Bill Riggs looked at him calmly, patted the Winchester in his hand. 'On the way, are they?' he commented. 'Good. I did a last round-up of the people who're willing to meet the Seatons. All the bank staff are armed and not one of them wants to duck out of the fight. The other townsmen are ready, too, so Santa Carmelita should give the Seatons the same kind of welcome the folks of the Wyoming town gave that gang who went in looking for trouble some time back.' He raised the Winchester in the air and added, 'And I'll have a chance to find out if these new-fangled babies are as good as they're cracked up to be.'

Riggs grinned in a way that suggested he was anticipating a fight with relish, then his face altered when he saw the vision that abruptly appeared in the street doorway. It was his daughter, Rosemary, but not the Rosemary of the essentially feminine neat shirtwaist and stylish full skirt. Now she was in a man's working shirt, blue jeans and a wide-brimmed sombrero. There was a shell belt around her slender waist and a Colt .45 in its holster. She wore the weapon in a way that indicated she knew how to use it.

Riggs stared hard at her and spluttered, 'What the Sam Hill are you in that get-up for?'

She gave him an impish grin and looked very different from the staid and rather off-putting personality whom Calland had first encountered.

'Why, Dad, can't you guess? I'm spoiling for a fight. The whole town is buzzing with the rumour that the Seaton outfit is on the way to make trouble and you have most of the men ready to fight them off. You don't imagine I want to be left out, do you?' she said.

'Damn it, girl, when I left home I said there was likely to be some shooting sooner or later and I told you to stay off the street.'

Rosemary grinned again and said, as if chiding a child, 'Now, Dad, don't go getting all red in the face. You taught me to shoot when I was no bigger than a shoe-button. You always said it was no bad thing for a girl to know how to handle weapons in this country. Mother was always proud of you as a law officer but she worried about the shooting scrapes you got involved in. Well, I don't intend to sit at home worrying if the Seatons come in shooting. I want to be in on the action. I can't help being my father's daughter.'

Bill Riggs groaned. 'Why on earth didn't you go off

to college where you'd be safe?'

'No, Dad. I thought it better to stay with you if ever you needed a helping hand—and here I am.'

'There's every chance of a big ruckus coming up and it'll be no place for a girl,' Riggs insisted.

'You can't put me off. When I saw you lying in the street after that fellow took a shot at you, I vowed I'd never stand idly by if ever you were in such danger again and I aim to back you up now that the Seaton gang are coming at us,' Rosemary insisted.

'You went all around town, alerting the citizens to be ready for some pretty big trouble, and I'm a citizen, too, and I insist on doing my duty. I'll stay right here with you in the marshal's office.'

Marshal Bill Riggs blew out his cheeks in an expression of near despair and he shook his head.

With a note of capitulation in his voice he said, 'All right. I know you can shoot but don't make a target of yourself and you won't be in the office because *nobody* will. The Seatons will focus on its door, expecting lawmen to rush out of it because they'll think they're making a surprise attack. They don't know what advance intelligence we have.

'There are a bunch of the sworn deputies posted in the alley on the far side of the office. Dave Cox and Jack Grover are among them. Stick close to those two and follow their lead. They'll all come out fast in a flanking attack from an unexpected position while the gang are concentrating on the front of the office. Go and tell them I told you to join them—and watch your step!'

'Thanks, Dad. You've just collected the keenest volunteer in all Santa Carmelita!' she said. She turned for the door, wearing a radiant expression of triumph and caught sight of Deputy Frank Calland looking at her with his face reflecting bewildered fascination.

And the hitherto frosty Rosemary proved she was highly elated indeed. She displayed the vigorous energy almost to be expected in a girl with such magnificent copper coloured hair. And she startled Calland by winking at him!

CHAPTER SIX

GUN FURY COMES TO TOWN

Jay Seaton's lean frame was stretched lazily in the most comfortable spot he could find beside the waterhole and he was finishing a pungent Mexican cigarillo.

He looked as though he was totally relaxed but, when embarking on a mission of robbery, he could never keep inwardly calm. Like a general before a battle, he considered over and over what advantages the field of combat might give to his troops and what it offered to the enemy. He took the stub of his cigarillo from his lips and ground it into the sandy earth with his thumb

He turned to query Daggett, seated on a rock close to him. 'You said the marshal's office in this town is right across from the bank?'

'Sure, there's hardly more than a few yards between them.'

'Then I guess the marshal's office is likely to be

where the most danger will come from almost as soon as we go into action, depending how many deputies Riggs has in the place,' Seaton said. 'We'll need to give it some special attention.

'Daggett, you and Krebs and Tolliver keep the office covered from the moment we hit town. Concentrate on that office and nothing more. As soon as anyone comes out of the door—shoot. Keep the lawmen off to give us a chance to have those guarding the front of the bank to get into place, and those doing the inside work to get up the steps and into the premises.'

Daggett opened his mouth to speak, but thought better of it. All along, he had dreaded the raid on Santa Carmelita bank because he wanted to keep well clear of Marshal Bill Riggs for reasons that had their origins long before either of them came into Arizona.

He craved some way of getting out of the duty Jay Seaton had just saddled him with but he could see Seaton was in no mood to stand any dickering about it at this late stage of the planned operation.

Seaton glowered at Daggett as if he sensed some spirit of reluctance in him and he said forcefully, 'And when I say shoot, Daggett, I mean shoot to kill. Cutting loose on some damned fool of a bank teller is plain dumb but when a man puts on a star and takes an oath to uphold the law, he makes himself an enemy of our kind, so he's fair game.'

Seaton stood up and called the gang to gather

around him. For the final time, he ran through the specific tasks allocated to each man. He urged quicker travel after this restful session and, when it was in the saddle, the band traversed the desert flats at a smarter rate.

Standing at the edge of town where the main street began and shielding his eyes, Frank Calland was the first to the see the swirls of risen dust on the far desert, the initial sign of a body of riders coming at some speed.

'They're coming—and pretty damned fast!' he reported urgently.

'Good,' said Bill Riggs. 'Let's get up on the roof. I'll fire the warning shot the minute they hit the edge of town. Our people are all in place, ready to welcome them.'

It was understood that Riggs and Calland would position themselves on the roof of the marshal's office and Riggs, from this vantage point, would fire once to announce the gang's arrival and set Santa Carmelita's defenders into blazing action.

The two lawmen lay on the flat roof of the office, both cradling Winchester carbines and keeping back from the edge of the roof so they could not be spotted from ground level.

Marshal Bill Riggs, who knew of Jay Seaton's reputation for meticulous planning, had laid out his own defensive strategy. The reliable volunteer deputies, plus

Rosemary, were out of sight in the alley on the further side of the door of the marshal's office and most were armed with the carbines from the rack in the office. Every upper and lower window and every store front in the vicinity of the bank had its concealed citizen with a ready rifle or revolver. On several roofs, armed men lay flat, out of the sight of those on the ground.

In his office, not far from the bank, old Doc Chivers sat with his medical bag to hand. He had checked over its contents of instruments and supplies, knowing he would be much in demand before the day was out.

In another office, lawyer Abe Scattergood checked the chambers of two Navy Colts, watched by his nephew, the supercilious Tobe Terrell.

'Surely you're not getting involved in this wild running around town in a blind panic with all these half-witted folks who are arming themselves to the teeth,' observed Terrell.

Scattergood had lost patience with the younger man and he faced him with a frown as dark as a thundercloud.

'I'm not running around in a panic,' he said sharply. 'I'm standing with this town in the face of a threat. I'm still the man who was a major in a Pennsylvania cavalry unit and I'm not scared of a fight. I used a pair of revolvers in a trick we learned from the Confederates in the war—fighting from the saddle with a pair of pistols. I'll be down there near the bank when needed.

And let me give you some advice, Tobe. I know your head is full of crazy ideas about the marshal and others being in the swim with the anti-Union moves in the South, but you're wrong. If you want to practice law here, you'll have to ante up and respect these folks. Make sure they trust you or they'll go to Tucson or elsewhere for a lawyer. Meantime, get yourself a gun and don't just sit on the fence in the upcoming ruckus.'

Terrell looked at his uncle dumbly and rubbed his chin. He was full of prejudices and he was absolutely certain that the shot fired at Marshal Bill Riggs missed him widely and that Riggs was play acting when he fell to the ground. He was still convinced that Riggs wanted to draw attention away from the man who fired on him to give him time to make his escape. Nevertheless, he had to admit his uncle was right and it would do him no good professionally to be an odd man out in a town like Santa Carmelita.

He left the office and returned to his room in the town's hotel where he kept a Colt .45 in a drawer.

All in Santa Carmelita were on high alert. The womenfolk, with the exception of Rosemary Riggs, sat anxiously behind the shutters of their homes. Their men, so many of whom a decade before had fought each other at Bull Run, Shiloh Church and on the bloody fields of Gettysburg, stood ready in common cause against those who would create mayhem in the peace all had craved.

*

The advancing gang came nearer to the town, riding in three ranks at a steady clip. All had their faces masked by bandanas, and the scorching sun put a glitter on their assortment of warlike trappings: Henry and Winchester carbines, full shell belts across their chests and holstered handguns. Jay Seaton rode in the front rank. His skinny body bestowed on him the suggestion of a dangerous snake and he displayed a vicious eagerness to be active in villainy.

His frame of mind had grown in its ugliness in the years since his band of renegade Southern soldiery ranked with their brother killer bands led by Quantrill, Todd and Anderson.

Also in the leading rank rode Cal Daggett, who now wished he was anywhere but in his present position. His bandana was very firmly in place and he hoped he could keep well out of the sight of Marshal Bill Riggs of Santa Carmelita. Ever since his fleeting encounter with the lawman during his scouting expedition in the town, Riggs had haunted his dreams like a dangerous spectre. If he had his way, he would bolt like a jackrabbit for the distant hills but he was totally in the grasp of Jay Seaton and he had to go through with his part in this raid.

Alongside him rode the pair detailed to partner him in the task of eliminating any danger from the marshal's office, Charlie Tolliver and Lou Krebs, two of the hardest cases and best shots in the whole Seaton outfit.

Jittering behind a heat haze, the first buildings of Santa Carmelita rose up in the path of the riders who were now only two minutes or so from entering the main street.

Seaton turned his head and growled to the whole contingent, 'All right, get your weapons ready. We're almost in town. Remember, our targets are right at the start of the street—bank at the left and the marshal's office directly across, to the right. You all know your jobs—let's get to it!'

Seaton spurred his horse, sending the animal plunging forward and he and the whole Seaton bunch surged into the first couple of feet of the main street, with the two key buildings in their view.

The crack of a Winchester shattered the stillness. Cal Daggett heard a brief gulping sound. He looked to his left and he saw Lou Krebs lurching back, dead in his saddle with a star-like splotch of crimson in his forehead.

The shot seemed to come from nowhere and it sent shock jarring through Daggett's innards. Then he saw a wisp of gun smoke curling up above the roof of the marshal's office. He lurched to one side, realizing that whoever was shooting from the roof had a plain advantage. The sniper need hardly show himself except when he let off a shot and he was shooting down on a crowded scene of mounted men. It was as easy as shooting fish in a barrel.

Daggett did not know that there were two riflemen on the roof of the marshal's office nor did he know that the first shot was the signal for the hidden defenders to emerge and open a storm of action. Windows in the bank and in buildings along the street and the storefronts suddenly became full of men wielding firearms. The alleyway beyond the marshal's office abruptly disgorged its squad of defenders who came out shooting. Up on the roof, Frank Calland fired a second Winchester blast at the now lurching and plunging mass of horsemen. Another couple of men fell from their saddles.

Up on the roof, Calland crawled precariously near the edge with his Winchester, drew a bead on a dimly discerned, pistol-firing marauder in the midst of the action at ground level. He squeezed the trigger and tough Charlie Tolliver slumped lifeless in his saddle.

Bill Riggs, lying beside Calland, showed his dogged determination, coolly pumping and triggering his Winchester at the invaders almost nonchalantly.

There was now chaos in the area at one end of the street. In a rapidly gathering fog of gun smoke, alarm began to possess the Seatons. Nothing of the slickly organized strategy devised by Jay Seaton had been put into action. It had been surmised that the gang would have the easy success it had in earlier lightning swift raids on unsuspecting townships. Seaton planned to have, in a matter of minutes, the lawmen of Santa Carmelita eliminated or, at least pinned down in their headquarters; the squad of dangerous guards covering the front of the bank while his select crew of speedy robbers were in the premises, grasping a haul of money. Instead, everything had started to come to pieces from the minute they set foot in the town.

To the raiders, it seemed that determined gun hands, firing every kind of weapon, had appeared as if by magic.

In fact, a whole cross-section of the population of Santa Carmelita was either involved in the action or hurrying to do so.

In his hotel room, the lawyer Tobe Terrell who felt himself to be far superior to the local people whom he saw as grubby yokels, many of whom were probably treasonable, looked from his window. He saw a billow of smoke drifting up from the other end of town and heard the racket of sustained gunfire. He saw the elderly telegrapher, Sim Jones, carrying a carbine and hurrying down the street in the direction of the battle. He was followed by a number of men, even youths and some excitable young boys.

A group of women, mostly carrying blankets and bowls and intent on dealing with the injured, rushed along in the wake of the men.

Terrell did not know why but he underwent a form

of on the spot conversion. He hastened to his bedside table, opened its drawer and produced his holstered Colt revolver attached to a folded shell belt. He belted the gun gear around his middle and hurried out of the door.

Out on the street, something quite unknown to the Seaton gang in all its long history of lawlessness was taking hold of its members—outright panic.

Seaton saw at once that the whole town appeared to have formed a deadly, impervious front against the raiders. Wild-eyed and in a cold sweat, he displayed a wholly new persona to his usual one of a cold commander who directed the delivery of wholesale death. He bellowed harsh commands to retreat which were hardly heard over the constant, crashing barrage of gunfire from the town's defenders.

At the same time, he strove to turn his horse and back out of the turbulent mass of frightened animals and panicking men. He saw a further couple of his men drop from their saddles and there were faces distorted with terror all around him.

Seaton spat and growled lurid oaths as he realized that men who had followed him in the dangerous ventures of wartime and in one audacious robbery after another, were turning yellow.

Over near the marshal's office, Cal Daggett, with his Colt in one hand, was trying to control his frightened mount. He was fearful of the bullets coming from the roof and from the squad of marshals that had emerged from the alleyway. He wanted to turn the animal and run for safety but the press of riders around him was crowding in on him. All had the same idea and were getting in the way of each other in a knot of sweating, bewildered horses and men who were gripped by terror.

Daggett was scared but his instinct of self-preservation still urged him to fight back at those who were attacking him. He fired a wild pistol shot at the group that had so swiftly emerged from the alley, dimly seen beyond the swirling blue smoke.

Jay Seaton, meantime, had faced down the panic that was threatening to override his normal cool management of a shooting spree. He somehow calmed his horse in the noisy chaos surrounding it and quickly dismounted. Bending almost double, he managed to unbuckle a bulky saddle bag and took from it the carefully guarded means of opening a stubborn iron safe—the squat wooden gunpowder keg with a quick fuse trailing from it. He had intended to enter the bank with the pair detailed to concentrate on the safe and use the explosive if other methods of cracking it failed.

With high anxiety clutching his guts, he scooted forward carrying the keg, found a space on the surface of the street that was free of trampling horses and surging, shooting men. He planted the keg in it and, with his heart in his mouth, fumbled in his pockets for a packet of Lucifer matches. He found it and struck a match on the emery strip on the packet. The match flared and Seaton touched the light to the fuse. If the Seaton outfit was about to meet its demise in Santa Carmelita, he was going to make sure the town knew it had been there.

His war experiences had taught Seaton the trick of separating himself from all that was going on around him, even if all hell was breaking loose, and concentrating on whatever task he had in hand. He disregarded the bullet-bitten chaos. He rushed back into the mêlée, bawling hoarsely to his men to retreat. He found his half-distracted horse, mounted, still yelling over the continuing gunfire. He turned the horse and spurred it out of the maelstrom of the fight.

Cal Daggett was riding low in his saddle and exchanging shots with the marshals, who were holding hard to their position beyond the curtain of powder smoke. He saw a figure among them fall, seemingly, a slim young man in a broad sombrero. Then he had the sudden, grotesque and chilling feeling that his victim was not a man at all but a young woman.

Immediately, Daggett's attention was taken by another of the defenders who came out of the smoky mist: an elderly looking man on horseback who charged forward, holding the rein between his teeth. He employed a method of fighting devised in the Civil

War by the troopers of the South's thrusting cavalry commander, Nathan Bedford Forrest, firing two pistols while galloping.

Daggett heard the cry of a stricken bandit and the agonized, snorting squeal of an injured horse but all other sounds were deadened by Jay Seaton's harsh command to retreat. He managed to turn his horse at last and spurred it to force it through the now disintegrating tangle of Seaton's band. With his rein between his teeth, lawyer Abe Scattergood controlled his horse by the touch of his spurs and caused it to prance around the fringe of the hectic commotion in front of the bank.

His sober legal persona was shed and his blood was up. He felt the old thrill he knew in the big War when, on the precarious border between living and dying, he went into action as a cavalryman.

Hardly five minutes before, Frank Calland came down from the roof of the office by the external stairway in the alleyway in which the marshals and Rosemary Riggs had gathered. He was followed by Bill Riggs. Both were still carrying their Winchesters and they now sought to add their weight to the furious welter of activity down at street level.

Just as the pair emerged from the alley into the chaotic, smoky street, he saw Rosemary suddenly break loose from the company of the marshals with whom she was fighting. Several paces from them, she halted and stood firing her Winchester into the midst of the roiling mass of raiders and animals, who were now hardly firing back but making desperate attempts to whirl around and quit Santa Carmelita. But one masked marauder, sprawling low in his saddle, fired and Calland watched in horror as the marshal's daughter scooted back on her heels, dropped her carbine, staggered and fell forward to hit the street.

Calland dropped his own carbine and rushed forward to reach the girl, then saw that she had fallen next to a horrifying object—a keg of gunpowder with a fizzing short fuse.

He lurched forward.

Almost sprawling on the keg, he grabbed it, straightened up, whirled and forced his way through struggling men and animals and hurled the keg into a clear portion of the street with all his strength.

As soon as it hit the earth, it exploded in a vivid flash of crimson and yellow flame with the report of a small cannon. Calland felt the blowback of the blast, wobbled on his feet but gathered his wits to turn and stagger back in search of Rosemary.

She was lying in the hoof-mauled dust, in the midst of struggling men and horses and in imminent danger of being trampled by distracted animals or scuffling boots. He bent, lifted her and, aware that a bullet might hit him at any moment, staggered back through the choking smoke.

Abruptly, he realized that Marshal Bill Riggs had appeared behind him, running backwards and covering the flight of his burdened deputy with his Winchester trained on the body of outlaws who were now hastening to quit the scene of their defeat.

Calland reached a space clear of the mass of men and mounts, pressed on, rubber legged as a drunkard, to reach the plank sidewalk outside a set of stores and laid the girl gently on it.

Riggs, with his begrimed face showing his anxiety, knelt with his deputy beside the stricken girl. Blood was seeping around her left shoulder, making her shirt sodden.

'Got to get her to Doc Chivers,' panted Riggs brokenly. 'My God, Frank, I'll never forget what you did with that keg of powder. I'll never know how to thank you for saving my girl.'

A tall man in a crumpled city suit came out of the dark, swirling murk of the smoke. He was carrying a Colt which he hastily shoved into the holster at his belt. He looked at Rosemary, seemed to quickly understand the urgency of the situation and said, 'I last saw Doc a little way along the street just back of here. He's working hard, dressing wounds. The mayor's wife is helping him. She was a nurse in the War.'

The young lawyer, Tobe Terrill, had been embroiled in the thick of the fighting and he now turned to re-enter it as it reached its dying stages.

The outlaws' attack on the town had overturned Terrill's prejudiced view of Santa Carmelita and its citizens. Contrary to his earlier prophesy, when the chips were down, the people had not showed themselves to be yellow. The vitality of their united, fighting front against the invading marauders suddenly converted him. He saw that he too belonged in the town and the knowledge brought out in him the gallantry of his father, the Union officer Major Joshua Terrill. He joined in the fighting with the same undaunted spirit as his uncle, Abe Scattergood, who battled in so unexpected a fashion.

Calland and Riggs between them carried the girl out of the deadly uproar that had turned the main street into a battleground, taking her further back along the street away from the immediate smoky storm near the entrance to the town. Her face was pale under the besmirching smoke of the battle and it was difficult to see whether she was breathing or not. The splotch of blood on her shirt close to her left shoulder seemed to be growing. Both men feared she was losing blood at a dangerous rate.

'By God, if she's dead, I'll never forgive myself for letting her get involved in this damned ruckus,' said Riggs in a choked voice.

In the quieter zone of the street, they found Doc Chivers conducting emergency doctoring on the wounded. He was being helped by the mayor's wife.

The doctor looked up from completing the bandaging of a man's hand, saw Rosemary's situation, pursed his lips and frowned.

'She needs treatment, for sure, Doc,' said Riggs anxiously.

'I can see that,' said Doc Chivers. 'Lay her down on the sidewalk and I'll get right to her.'

Riggs and Calland laid the girl on the planks and Mrs Cotton, the mayor's wife, came over to help the doctor.

'She'll live, Marshal, but I'll have to stitch the wound,' the doctor reported.

'I saw the man who shot her,' stated Frank Calland gravely as Doc Chivers bent over the marshal's daughter. 'It was the one who fired on you, Marshal. The one I met on the desert, the one called either Beale or Daggett.'

Riggs looked up from where he knelt beside Rosemary. 'You did? How could you recognize him? Every man jack of the Seaton crew was heavily masked up to the eyes.'

'I knew him by his clothes,' responded Calland. 'Same hat, same shirt, everything he wore was just the same as when I first met him near Stone Creek City.'

'I'll kill him!' vowed Riggs, with a slightly crazed note in his voice. 'By God, if I get my hands on him, I'll kill him!'

The fighting at the further end of the street was

now rapidly subsiding and the deputies who had been in the alleyway led by the bulky restaurant owner, Dave Cox, came up and crowded around the stricken girl with their faces reflecting their concern.

'Sorry this has happened, Marshal,' said Cox. 'We kept an eye on her but she was feisty as all get-out and there was no holding her once Seaton's mob hit town. She got her dander up and jumped into the fight before anyone could stop her.'

Mayor Amos Cotton came into the group holding a Winchester with which he had taken an active part in the battle. He looked at Rosemary with concern. 'After Doc finishes, take her over to my house and my wife will look after her.'

'Sure, Marshal, I'll take good care of her,' said Mrs Cotton. 'Don't you worry about her.'

The lawyer Abe Scattergood, blackened by smoke and breathless and now dismounted, arrived.

'What's left of the Seaton gang has run for it,' he reported. 'They turned tail and scooted out of town after the explosion, with Seaton in the lead. They left some behind, maybe four dead and a couple wounded and some dead horses, too. Two or three townsfolk were hurt in that blast and it damaged part of the front of the bank and the marshal's office.'

'By thunder I'll make them pay!' growled Riggs savagely. 'Not just for Rosemary but for that powder keg trick.'

A makeshift litter was provided and Rosemary was carried to Doc Chivers's office where he could carry out the stitching under suitable conditions. Bill Riggs and Calland left Riggs's daughter, still unconscious, in the doctor's premises. She lay on the table on which the doctor performed operations.

Doc Chivers and Mrs Cotton washed their hands and methodically selected instruments from a cabinet.

Down at the location of the battle, the two lawmen briefly visited the scene outside the bank where they found the bodies of four of the raiders and a couple of the gang sitting in the dust dejectedly nursing wounds. Three townsfolk were killed by the powder explosion and others who had been blown off their feet and stunned by it were sitting around, recovering. Willing helpers were damping down the slight fires caused by the exploding keg at the front of some of the buildings nearest the blast.

Marshal Bill Riggs kept his sense of urgency and his burning desire to avenge the injury of his daughter and the damage to the town tightly battened down as he gathered the group of sworn deputies around him and issued orders for restoring order.

The surviving raiders were arrested and housed in the cells of the marshal's office until Doc Chivers could attend to their wounds after he finished his emergency work on Rosemary Riggs.

Calland was left to check on those who had

responded with hot lead from the windows of the bank and the various other buildings, ensuring there were no deaths or serious wounds, as well as organizing a general clean-up of the scene of battle. After calling at Sim Jones's telegraph office to send a report on the action at Santa Carmelita to the federal marshal at Tucson and arrange the setting up of trials for the prisoners, Bill Riggs returned to the doctor's quarters and found Rosemary had been removed to the mayor's home where she was under the care of Mrs Cotton.

Doc Chivers said he had arrested the loss of blood and the patient was now conscious. To Riggs's relief, he reported that her general prognosis was good.

At Mayor Cotton's house, Riggs discovered Rosemary weak, with her shoulder tightly bandaged but she was in bright spirits. He found out she had been rendered unconscious by a bullet that had merely creased her scalp but Chivers had stitched the slight wound and she was feisty as ever, rejoicing at the vanquishing of Jay Seaton and his gang.

Considerably heartened, Riggs returned to pressing duties. The remnants of the raiders, about eight in all, including Seaton, had scooted out into the desert and had a start over any pursuers. But Riggs took comfort from the fact that their horses had first made a long journey out of Mexico, then endured the exhausting experience of the riot before the defenders of Santa Carmelita. They were bound to tire swiftly where a posse from the town would start out on fresh mounts.

The marshal's desire to visit dire retribution on Jay Seaton and the remainder of his gang was intensified by the injury of his daughter through her participation in the battle on the street, and he blamed himself for allowing her to join the townsfolk in resisting the raiders.

But a less emotional part of his consciousness told him that, even if he had forbidden her participation, her spirit was such that she would have defied him and made sure she was in the fight.

Riggs's initial anger had now lost its edge and he went about forming his posse with a cold logic. Although numerous townsmen wanted to participate, he selected men he knew were fitted for a possibly gruelling expedition in search of the marauders. He took Frank Calland, knowing his military experience on the desert, and Jack Grover the gunsmith who had a reputation as a marksman; six of his volunteer marshals whom he knew had wartime experience with both armies and a further couple of hardy citizens whom he reckoned had the stamina to withstand rigorous journeying in unfriendly country.

They were a company of stolid men of varying ages from frontier veterans to younger men like Ed Corbett, a volunteer from the bank where he was a teller. He was an athletic Easterner of intellectual tastes and of somewhat mysterious background. He was reputed to have had a high-class education.

Dave Cox, of the eating house, wanted to justify his volunteer deputy's star and join the posse but Bill Riggs introduced a rare touch of humour, telling him he'd be doing a more valuable service by readying meals for a population hungering for after-the-battle sustenance and his wife's celebrated apple pie.

'And you'd better rustle up some solid saddle rations for the posse, Dave. There's no telling how long we'll be out in the desert,' he said.

Another hopeful who was turned away was lawyer Tobe Terrell who had been through a process of metamorphosis, losing his dandified manners through his blooding in the harsh realities of frontier living— and dying. He now looked—and felt—that he really belonged in Santa Carmelita. He had even forgotten the intriguing question of why Marshal Bill Riggs fell to the ground when the bullet fired at him missed him widely.

'Sorry, Mr Terrell,' said Riggs, 'but may I suggest you go through your law books to discover how many charges we can arraign on what's left of the Seaton bunch? Because we will bring them in sure enough!'

When the posse was ready with saddled horses, food supplied by Dave Cox, newly charged firearms and full water canteens, the marshal's office was left in the care of the remaining marshals. They had the duties of guarding the prisoners, ensuring that their wounds were dealt with by Doc Chivers when he had attended to the stricken townsfolk and that they were fed, again with Dave Cox supplying the menu.

A last minute conference on strategy was held by the posse in the marshal's office with the group standing around a large map of the region unfolded on Bill Riggs's desk. Frank Calland, who had most recently experienced conditions on the Mexican trail, pointed to the waterhole where he had observed the gang on their inward journey.

'They've most likely passed this point by now unless they're slowed up by tired horses and we don't know if they have any wounded with them to hinder them,' he said. 'It's likely they have very little grub, if any. If they lingered too long at the waterhole we might come within sight of them. There's no other place they can stop for water until they reach this hole here, which is nearly on the Mexican line.' He stabbed the map with his forefinger.

'My guess is they'll stick to the trail because it'd be senseless to go off it. On the desert, there are no towns, settlements or any place they can find water or food.

'There's only a spot well off the trail here, marked as "Abandoned Indian ruins", which usually means crumbling adobe huts hundreds of years old. No, their only hope is to stay right on the trail all the way to Mexico, weary horses and all. We'll keep right behind them and nail them—and the odds are stacked in our favour.'

The posse swung into their saddles just as that eventful day stretched into late afternoon, reminding the avenging riders that night would enfold the desert wastes before they returned to Santa Carmelita.

Frank Calland, whose mount was next to Bill Riggs's, saw the marshal spin the chambers of his Colt Peacemaker and noted his expression of grim determination. He was doubtless thinking of his daughter, lying injured at Mayor Cotton's home. Calland had also had her on his mind ever since the fighting in the town ceased.

He could not forget how her earlier frosty demeanour gave way to a spirited feistiness and how he saw her as a different girl when she so audaciously winked at him just before she plunged into the battle against the Seaton gang.

CHAPTER SEVEN

FUGITIVES FROM VENGEANCE

Jay Seaton was fuming. He was leading seven riders, the remnant of his gang of fourteen, and his scarecrow lean figure was almost quivering in the saddle with rage.

Never in his long career of lawlessness had he ever suffered such humiliation and frustration and such a merciless whipping as he and his band had encountered at Santa Carmelita.

Seaton's risky planting of the powder keg in the midst of the bullet-trading fight was partly through desperation at not being able to get into the bank, and partly through a vindictive desire to strike a hard blow at the town that had turned the tables on his gang's long career of spectacular criminal infamy.

The origins of the Seaton outfit were rooted in the fast moving, mounted guerrilla bands of the Southern Confederacy, in the Civil War, some of whom had only a tentative association with the army of the South while others were eventually disowned by the Confederacy. They burned and plundered towns in the Missouri and Kansas region, known for their anti-slavery stance; they raided Union Army supply lines and troop trains; waylaid troops on the march; shot and hanged unarmed civilians and committed all manner of atrocities.

It became a habit which could not be shaken off by many participants who remained uncaptured and unhanged at the close of the war and who had vowed never to knuckle down to the rule of the victorious North. They turned wartime raiding to profit in the uneasy post-War days. Banks in new frontier towns and trains carrying consignments of money were prey to the marauding bands of which the Seaton outfit had earned the most feared reputation.

Jay Seaton, backed by a lawless group containing many who rode with him in the bloodthirsty War years, thought he had perfected the techniques of bank robbery. His carefully planned forays in search of loot grabbed at gunpoint had paid off handsomely all along the frontier for nearly a decade after the War.

The Seatons had figured the tried and trusted plan of swift action that had worked so well at Stone Creek City and other settlements would work just as smoothly at another sleepy desert town but Santa Carmelita turned out to be not so sleepy. Its fighting citizenry matched the folks of the town in Wyoming where the grasping gang led by the Prothero brothers met its destruction. And all the Seaton gang's planning had not brought in a single stolen cent!

Among the seven riding at Seaton's back was Cal Daggett, counting himself lucky to have escaped with a whole skin. Weighing heavily on Daggett's mind was the worry that, almost certainly, Marshal Bill Riggs would bring a posse in pursuit of the last of the Seaton outfit. And, after the destruction wrought at the town, it was likely to be a big posse, looking for vengeance without any half measures.

Having avoided any direct contact with Riggs in the Santa Carmelita raid, for reasons originating long before, he had no desire to meet him in a close-quarters encounter on the desert. He did not know that the young woman he shot at Santa Carmelita was the marshal's daughter or that a furious Riggs nursed a blazing desire to inflict retribution on him.

Furthermore, Daggett was aware that Jay Seaton seemed not to fully trust him ever since his disappearance after the raid at Stone Creek City, and he rode in stolid silence, having earlier caused Seaton's tetchy keg temper to flare.

The current defeated condition of the remains of Seaton's band did not suit Daggett one iota. Events at Stone Creek City and Santa Carmelita would ensure the widespread posting of rewards, and every law enforcement officer throughout Arizona Territory and beyond would be itching to get his hands on the Seaton gang. Daggett felt the bunch had played its last hand. He hankered to cut loose and gallop at break-neck speed for the far horizon.

Jay Seaton also was plagued by nagging worries. Among them was a conviction he shared with Daggett that Marshal Bill Riggs, of the frontier-wide reputation, was sure to be in pursuit with a vengeance hungry posse. He was concerned too, about what the prisoners taken at Santa Carmelita would reveal to the questioning officers of the law. How much would they tell of the gang's past activities? Would they name gang members hitherto unknown to the authorities, putting their names on the hangman's rope?

Then there was the disturbing matter of Nebraska Carlsen.

Two of the riders were carrying flesh wounds which doubtless required attention but a fourth, the bulky Nebraska Carlsen, who once functioned as the gang's cook, was severely stricken. He was shot in the stomach by defenders of the bank and a gut-shot was among the worst wounds a man might suffer in an environment where surgery was crude, even if attainable.

In addition, the big man had a wound in the arm to which his colleagues had applied an inadequate bandage. This failed to stem the flow of blood which dripped down his sleeve, down his clothing and saddle trappings and sometimes to the trail.

Nebraska Carlsen scarcely knew where he was, He was slumped, semi-conscious, in his saddle with his head drooping forward while his horse kept pace with the other animals through instinct.

There were dark thoughts concerning Nebraska Carlsen among some of his colleagues who had queasy guts through sheer fear. He was so badly wounded most felt he must surely die though no one put that thought into words. He was plainly a burden and there were those who secretly wished he could simply be left beside the trail so the others might hasten their flight out of the United States territory and into Mexico.

But ditching an injured colleague was not Jay Seaton's style, in spite of all his brutality and his fear, and any suggestion that it be done would not sit well with him. In fact, it would certainly touch off his present darkly brooding and defeated mood into blazing fury. Seaton had his own peculiar sense of honour and his own code of ethics.

For him, the gang, rooted in the fast moving guerrilla units, still represented the defiant and diehard Southern spirit. They rode roughshod over the law they despised as Yankee law, fashioned in Washington. In his view, they still served the old flag of the South even though the embarrassed and ashamed government of that flag had disowned many of their kind while the War still raged.

In Seaton's twisted view, the old rebel bands of his

kind, now outlawed, had the right to be treated as heroes.

There was little heroic spirit among his dejected followers. This was late afternoon and nothing could be surer than the fact that a posse from Santa Carmelita must be on their tails. Prospects of eluding it were not bright and the fleeing Seaton riders knew their horses were already weary through that day's hard riding from Mexico and strenuous usage in the battle of Santa Carmelita.

The gang's remnant had yet to reach the waterhole and Cal Daggett, knowing the ability of the Santa Carmelita men to attack with determined fire power, did not relish the prospect of being caught by the posse on the open trail. It dawned on him that, at the waterhole, they would have the cover of rocks and vegetation and might make a stand against the avenging horsemen. It seemed logical to Daggett, in spite of his secret wish for an opportunity to cut and run from what remained of the Seaton gang. His loyalty to the outfit was beginning to be frayed even at the time of the raid in Stone Creek City.

In fact, all the suspicions of Jay Seaton about Daggett's behaviour at Stone Creek City were true. With a bad attack of jitters after shooting the bank teller, he panicked and attempted to desert which led to his meeting with Frank Calland. Then he remembered the safety of running with the pack and made his furtive return, showing up at the Mexican bolthole.

The subsequent chance encounter with Bill Riggs and the fiasco at Santa Carmelita further unnerved him. Now, out on the desert with the gang's limping survivors, weary horses, no supplies and with a posse assuredly pursuing, he had an acute itch to quit all over again. He had no appetite for an exchange of hot lead with a group led by dogged Bill Riggs, whom he desired to avoid at all costs. If Riggs and his men were to be faced, however, it surely stood to reason to hunker down and fight them off from a place offering adequate cover.

He called to Seaton, riding at the head of the group, suggesting this course and was rewarded by the rough edge of the outlaw chief's tongue.

Seaton turned his head and growled harshly, 'Nothing doing! We'll linger at the waterhole only long enough to refresh ourselves and the horses. We will not set ourselves up for another whipping. You sorry bunch gave in too easy back in Santa Carmelita. You backed out quick when that bunch of yokels started to shoot without fighting back the way you should. You never attempted to get into the bank.'

He seemed to have totally forgotten his own actions in urging a retreat in the face of the withering fire or the solid defence of the townsfolk. Nor did he remember that the strong and deadly opposition prevented any chance to enter the bank His attitude seemed half-crazed, for there had been no hope of ever putting the whole, carefully worked out robbery plan into action,

It dawned on Daggett that, as much of his followers, Seaton was running scared but managing to keep the lid on his panic.

So they made their sullen way towards the waterhole as the first touches of evening darkened the wide sky, shadowing their unprepossessing faces. There was Daggett, sly-eyed and cunning, eager to be anywhere but on the trail with the certainty of pursuit by Bill Riggs. There was the hefty Dan Forrest, with half his face covered by a black beard, who growled with the pain of a bullet-nicked leg. Skinny Dick Filson was also injured with a flesh wound in the arm. Ed Deems and Nick Drago, always a silent, brooding pair, had hard-bitten, sullen faces, at all times unrevealing of what was going through the brains of either man. Frenchy de Courcey, with his lantern-jawed face begrimed by powder smoke, looked anything but the scion of an aristocratic Louisiana family he claimed to be and there was the near comatose Nebraska Carlsen, slumped in his saddle with his nearest companions occasionally ensuring he was still upright.

When almost within sight of the waterhole, Frenchy de Courcey, riding next to Carlsen, saw his head suddenly droop forward as he uttered a hardly audible, gasp. His body slid over to one side and de Courcey reached out to grasp his sleeve and haul him back. Half a minute later, de Courcey yelled over the heads of the riders in front of him, 'Jay! Nebraska's dead!'

'I figured that was about to happen,' responded Seaton without any emotion. 'We'll stop off at the waterhole and set about burying him.'

Dick Filson took a chance on sparking Seaton's temper, so explosive in the bandit chief's current jittery state. 'We can't hang around for too long, Jay,' he warned.

Like his companions, Filson hoped he might find a doctor in Mexico to tend his injured arm and did not want to tarry too long at the waterhole. Like his fellows, he could almost hear avenging hoofs drumming in their back trail.

'I know that, damn you!' Seaton barked. 'Nebraska rode with me in the War. He was a soldier of the Confederacy and he deserves a proper burial. I'm not leaving him so the coyotes and buzzards can get at him. Anyone who doesn't like it can keep riding for Mexico—the whole blasted lot of you can if you feel that way and I'll find a way of burying him myself.'

There was already a visitor to the waterhole who was alerted by the sound of approaching horsemen, a bent ancient man in ragged, sun-bleached clothing and with a scrubby bearded and deeply lined face under a severely punished old sombrero. He was accompanied by a burro, burdened by humped gunny sacks, a spade and various tin pans.

Old Elihu Meeks had been prospecting on the desert for so long even he could not recall a time when he was not trudging the wastes with only a burro for companionship.

He could remember his meagre successes but was not put off prospecting by the fact that they were very few and far between. Rather, he was buoyed by the belief that a small strike was evidence of a big one lying under the earth waiting to be discovered. All a man had to do was keep looking, keep hoping and keep digging.

The talk among desert men in those early 1870s was of silver being struck in southern Arizona and somebody, somewhere, was sure to find a lode that could keep him in luxury for evermore. Such talk goaded old Elihu to more trudging, more digging and more hoping.

For the moment, however, he was camped beside the waterhole, smoking his pipe while his burro, in the way of desert-bred animals, drank sparingly.

The tramp of hoofs and the jingle of ring bits startled Elihu out of a dreamy reverie in which he was overjoyed by the discovery of a bonanza: a record breaking mother lode of silver.

The old man rolled over from his sitting position to lie on his stomach and slither forward to peer through the coarse grass and fronds of ferns growing by the edge of the water.

A group of shadowy riders, led by a skinny man, were advancing through the gathering gloom.

In the failing light, Elihu took in the sight of their weaponry and he knew who they were. He had heard rumours out of Stone Creek City concerning the rampaging gang of bank robbers led by the notably thin Jay Seaton.

Old Elihu had lived a life of risk. He had risked the hazards of desert wanderings; a dozen or more dangers from thirst, searing sunstroke, attack by hostile Indians, blackwater fever and the uncountable chances a man took just by venturing into the company of his fellow human beings in brawling frontier towns.

There were those who might hold that, like many veteran desert denizens, he was slightly cracked through a lonely existence under a blazing sun but his long experience had bred in him a certain cavalier attitude towards men who had acquired dangerous reputations. He reasoned that if he was not perturbed by thirst, scorpions and rattlesnakes, why should he pay much heed to men who swaggered around armed to the teeth?

Consequently, as Seaton and his party neared the waterhole, he stood up to reveal himself and walked forward to plant himself in the path of the riders.

Jay Seaton reined up in front of the old man.

'Who're you?' he demanded.

'Just Elihu Meeks, an old coot of not much account. Leastways, that's the way I am right now. This time tomorrow, I'll probably be a millionaire. I aim to make a big strike of rich ore out on the desert pretty darned soon.'

Seaton gave a sardonic laugh. 'That's what all you old desert rats say,' he commented. He looked across at the waterhole and saw Elihu's heavily burdened burro standing in the shadows and said, 'If that's a shovel on the back of your animal, we'd like to borrow it.'

Elihu cast his eyes over the halted steeds and nodded towards the big form of Carlsen, slanted in his saddle.

'It'll be needful in the case of your big friend there,' he said. 'He looks dead to me. Better bury him before we have the turkey buzzards flapping over us.'

'We aim to,' said Seaton. He jerked his head towards the water as a wordless command and the riders swung out of their saddles and scrambled off to slake their thirst and that of their horses.

Nick Drago buttonholed Elihu. 'You got any grub, old timer? Our bellies are getting empty,' he growled.

'Nary a bite. I ate the last of my beef jerky an hour ago,' said Elihu. 'I know where you can get some, though.'

'You do? Where?'

'About two miles due east,' said Elihu, pointing off the trail. 'There's an old Indian town, mostly in ruins.

118

A bunch of Indians are squatting there. They'll give you grub.'

'Indians? Hostiles?' echoed Drago, alarmed.

'No, they ain't hostiles. They're Pimas, and Pimas are friendly to white folks. I know them well. They're a long way from their own country, down by the Salt River. I reckon they skipped over this way to escape being put on the reservation and the army ain't caught them yet.'

'Hear that, Jay?' shouted Drago to Seaton who was filling his canteen at the waterhole. 'There's a set of Pimas not far away. They're friendly and they can supply some grub.'

An answer came from Dan Forrest. 'Pimas be damned. I have a wounded leg and I need a doctor, so does Filson. If we hang around here too long we'll have a posse on our necks before we know it.'

'Shut up, Forrest!' interjected Seaton harshly.

He trudged back from the water to join Elihu Meeks and Drago. He had just been smitten by the notion that going off the trail to the Pima encampment could prove a cunning diversion. A Santa Carmelita posse would probably conclude that, having visited the water-hole, the Seaton party had stayed on the trail, heading for Mexico and they would keep on course in the same direction. After feeding and resting with the Pimas for a spell, the Seaton party might make a cautious return back over the border.

'Is what you're telling us true, old timer?' asked Seaton roughly. 'Or are you selling us out into the hands of a gang of hostile Indians? You know who we are, don't you? If you're playing a smart trick on us, by thunder, we'll catch up with you and make you regret it.'

'I know who you are and what I told you is true,' said Elihu indignantly. 'Why should I play games with you? I've nothing to gain. I haven't seen any big rewards posted for you and I don't care what's being offered. Why should I when I feel it in my bones that I'm about to strike a big bonanza on the desert any day now and I'll be richer than a king? And why do you think I took to the desert long ago? To get away from my fellow men, that's why.

'I want no truck with humanity, governments or law and order and all the shackles the authorities put on a man. I just want to be left to myself.'

Elihu paused for a moment then pointed to the desert beyond the waterhole. 'By the way,' he said, 'you have a couple of injured men. Well, the Pimas yonder have an old medicine man who's pretty good with the Indian style of doctoring. I was bitten by a sidewinder some years back and was damned sure I was a goner. I got myself to the Pimas and he did his stuff with herbs and potions. He cured me and getting a man to survive a sidewinder bite is damned near a miracle.'

Elihu watched the burial of Nebraska Carlsen on

the desert a short distance from the waterhole. It was done hastily without any form of ceremony, though Jay Seaton, with his tattered loyalty to the dead-and-gone Confederate States, would have preferred to have a military body fire, a farewell salute over the grave and a lowering of the Stars and Bars flag of the South.

At the close, Seaton gave the command to mount and ride. 'We're going off-trail to find the Pimas this old coot told us about to get some grub and this medical attention of theirs,' he stated.

Some discontentment with this move was reflected on the faces of various members of the group, as if they felt following the known path to Mexico was the better way despite the hazard of a pursuing posse. Taking to the trackless wilderness and seeking the aid of Indians who might not be wholly trusted could prove even more hazardous.

It was true that the Pima people were broadly friendly to settlers but there were some instances of belligerency on their part. In spite of the yarn told by the old desert rat, if the group squatting by the old ruins were truly dodging the authorities who would put them on a reservation, they might be just as resentful of a group of heavily armed outlaw intruders as they were of the US Army.

No objections were voiced, however, and the riders followed Jay Seaton, urging their mounts off the trail and into the darkening shades of the desert.

Old Elihu Meeks stood on the trail watching them go. As the last rider disappeared into the night, he gave a low, rumbling and sardonic chuckle.

CHAPTER EIGHT

BLOOD ON THE TRAIL

The Santa Carmelita posse came up the Mexico trail, keeping a steady pace so as not to tire their mounts too quickly. Riding at their head with Marshal Bill Riggs, Frank Calland kept both the wide vista of the desert and the trail immediately before the knot of riders under his searching gaze, So far as he could make it, it had an Indian's focus. Any glimmer of light on the far flats and any slight clue left by those who had travelled the trail before them might speak of the passage of the remnant of Jay Seaton's gang and of where they currently were.

Just as the afternoon had lengthened and the desert dusk was soon to settle on the panoramic landscape, Calland spotted a small, dark blob on the trail ahead of the leading horses, so small that a less acute scrutiny might easily have missed it. He raised his hand to signal a halt and the riders reined up.

Calland and Riggs dismounted and walked forward

to stoop and examine the marking of the trail. Close inspection revealed smaller spots around it. Calland touched the large spot. It was still moist.

'Blood!' pronounced Calland, showing his finger to Riggs. 'It's fairly fresh, too.'

Riggs nodded. 'It's blood, all right. It means at least one of them is wounded enough to bleed fairly freely. We've not yet hit the waterhole and they might still be there but I doubt if they'd be crazy enough to camp for long and light a fire. They'll have savvy enough to know all Santa Carmelita wants a final settlement with them and will have put a posse on their tail.'

The rest of the posse had left their saddles to stretch their legs and give their horses some respite and now formed a group around the lawmen.

'Better keep our eyes skinned from this point on,' warned Jack Grover, the gunsmith. 'I know the waterhole and, if they're there, they'll have sight of us arriving as we approach around the bend in the trail. Could be they'll have a lookout posted on the ridge above the waterhole but with night falling fast, he'll have a hard time seeing us.'

'So don't light up any smokes from here on in,' said Bill Riggs. 'The slightest light will give us away and I want to see this bunch mopped up for good and all.' There was bitter savagery in his tone. 'They came into my town and raised hell and they're going to learn hell in return—right to the hilt!'

They remounted and rode further as the light dwindled, and they were on the edge of night when another tell-tale blotch was seen on the trail, this time telling a more dramatic tale.

Calland, examining the surface of the trail again, reported, 'Whoever was hurt was in fairly bad shape— or maybe we are seeing evidence of more than one wounded man in their crew. Seems to me a wounded man, or more than one, would call for a lengthy stop at the waterhole if they were treating them as best they could and needing plenty of water. The waterhole is not far ahead, just around the bend.'

'We could surprise them unless they have some idea we're close behind them,' said Marshal Bill Riggs. 'Keep yourselves ready for some hard trading with bullets. This bunch will never submit to arrest. Every one of them knows he can expect nothing but the gallows and we know damned well how they can throw hot lead. Ride at a smart clip around that bend and don't holler or make too much noise. With luck we'll surprise them and settle their hash right smart.'

Riggs spurred his horse to take the lead. Calland rode beside him and the posse advanced quickly with firearms ready and only the drumming of hoofs to betray them. The posse rounded the bend and the spindly trees marking the source of the water came into view.

Also into view came the unexpected vision of

another traveller, coming in their direction. Shadowed by the falling night, it was a squat little man, walking and accompanied by a burro carrying a shapeless bundle.

Bill Riggs narrowed his eyes to peer through the uncertain light and gave a gasp of surprise.

'Well, can you believe it?' he exclaimed. 'Elihu Meeks, of all people!' He turned to Calland. 'Elihu is a diehard old prospector. He's been fossicking around the desert hereabout since time began. He visits every settlement around in these parts once in a while but he hasn't been in Santa Carmelita for some time.'

The marshal gave the signal to the posse to halt to allow the old man to reach them. He approached the leading riders cautiously, squinting at them to identify them then he cackled a laugh of recognition.

'Why it's Marshal Riggs and friends!' he declared. 'At first, I took you for another bunch of bad men. I'm on my way to hit Santa Carmelita in due course to collect some grub and tobacco.'

'Another bunch of bad men? Does that mean you met some on the trail?' asked Riggs.

'I'll say I did and I heard mention of a posse that might be hot on their tail. I know who they were, too. I recognized their skinny boss. It was that damned Jay Seaton and his crew. Looks like they were raising hell in Santa Carmelita if you're after them.'

'They were but they didn't get things all their own

way. Where did you meet them?'

With his thumb, Elihu indicated the trail at his back.

'At the waterhole, just a little way back there. They set off, travelling east from the waterhole about an hour and a half ago.'

The old man told how the fugitives went in search of food as well as help for their two injured men from the Pimas, squatting near the old ruins.

'Two are injured so how many are left?' asked Frank Calland.

'Seven including Seaton. There were eight when they arrived at the waterhole but one was dead in the saddle. They buried him. I counted them, figuring I'd meet you fellows and you'd want to know their strength. I played dumb and told that bunch of polecats I was no friend of law and order. I reckon they took me for an old crackpot—which I ain't.'

'I should say not, Elihu,' said Riggs. 'Thanks, you've done us a service, telling us they've taken to the desert. Otherwise, we'd have stuck to the trail, thinking they were ahead of us and bound for Mexico.'

'Good luck, Marshal. You should come across them tolerably easy. It's rough country between the trail and them old ruins and their cayuses looked plumb tuckered,' chuckled Elihu. 'I hope you give that Seaton crew a good whipping. They have no right picking on a respectable town like Santa Carmelita. Why, there are folks there that even respected a flea-bitten old gopher like me.'

The posse left Elihu to his trudging progress and headed for the waterhole.

A clear plan was in the mind of Marshal Bill Riggs. With the night advancing, they could eat and rest at the waterhole where their horses would find enough vegetation to crop. They could snatch some sleep knowing that Seaton and his companions would be fumbling in the darkness in unfamiliar and inhospitable country on horses that must be low on stamina. In the morning, they could start freshly charged for some rough travelling and standing every chance of coming upon the fugitives fairly quickly.

The waterhole site offered every opportunity for relaxation. A fire was lit, coffee was boiled and the Santa Carmelita men made a supper of the food they carried with them. When organizing the posse, Bill Riggs, with his meticulous attention to its needs, had thought of the possibility of spending nights on the trail and had insisted on bedrolls being packed.

A couple of men, changing at two hourly intervals throughout the night, kept watch in case the Seaton riders became frustrated with their difficult night journeying and found their way back to the known trail. But the night passed tranquilly and the posse was up, refreshed and active with the crack of dawn.

After eating, the men were securing their saddle

trappings and Bill Riggs was standing by his horse.

'Let's hope we have some advantage over the Seaton bunch with our horses and ourselves rested and fed. With luck, they've had a hard time in the darkness with no clear trail to follow,' he said to Calland. 'Could be we'll need those Indian tracking tricks you learned in the army, Frank, and the sooner we find them the sooner I can have the satisfaction of settling things with that snake Beale or Daggett or whatever he is calling himself.'

'You mean for shooting Rosemary?'

'Yes, for Rosemary,' replied Riggs. And he added darkly, 'For Rosemary and some other things.'

Frank Calland's mind went back to Riggs studying the reward flyer and the intense interest he showed in the robber. Then he thought of the presence in Santa Carmelita of the man he knew as Beale who had shot at Riggs and the marshal's odd behaviour, obstructing attempts to pursue Beale. His suspicion that there was something between the two men was revived by Riggs stating there were reasons other than the shooting of his daughter for his seeking a settlement with Beale/Daggett.

Calland probed no further, remembering Western tradition of not asking too many questions about a man's background since there might be aspects he wished to keep hidden. It was a tradition that had gathered weight since the Civil War.

As the posse set off to traverse the great, garish panorama of the open desert, Calland noted Riggs's silence and his grim, resolute expression, suggestive of a predatory animal scenting its quarry.

Calland felt the lust to kill was building in the marshal's heart with the man known as both Beale and Daggett as his prospective victim.

Just off the Mexico trail, the posse made the early discovery of fresh hoof tracks that were distinct for a good distance but it was not easy travelling for the posse. Lacking a distinct trail, they had to make their way over tangled terrain.

Occasionally, the hoof tracks were lost as the fugitives made diversions because they had encountered heaped boulders or tracts of thickly grown cactus and catclaw. Now and again, they were forced to cross long dried-out watercourses but Calland, dismounted and using the Indian tracking skills learned through desert soldiering, always rediscovered the trail.

'This country must have given them trouble aplenty in darkness,' commented Calland.

'It's my guess the going was too much for them and they pretty soon gave up and made a night camp then continued riding this morning. We can't be too far behind them.'

The posse headed onward for another half hour under a sun which was riding to its noon zenith. They came to some tall, sun-split boulders, almost blocking their way, with a scattering of smaller boulders at their base. Riggs raised his arm and called a halt.

'Look at what we have here,' he called as he and the party hauled their reins.

The posse stared ahead and saw a lone man emerging from the shelter of the larger boulders, a defeated looking figure, wearily picking his way over the lesser boulders. He held his upper right arm with his left hand as if trying to ease an injury and began to stagger towards the posse.

He reached Riggs and Calland in the lead of the group. He was obviously almost all-in. His right shirt sleeve was caked in congealed blood and his eyes glittered feverishly. He had a Colt .45 holstered at his thigh.

He looked at Riggs and Calland, obviously taking in the lawmen's stars and croaked a cracked greeting.

'I know who you are—you're the posse from Santa Carmelita,' he said hoarsely. 'I'm giving myself up. I'm Dick Filson and I've have had enough of running—'

He was interrupted by Bill Riggs, who had already drawn his Peacemaker, barking an order to the posse, 'Watch those boulders! This fellow could be a decoy!'

His followers had instinctively drawn their weapons the instant they spotted Filson but no shooting came from outlaws hidden in the boulders.

'I'm no decoy and this is no ambush,' croaked Filson. 'There's only one man in those boulders and that's Dan Forrest. He has a wounded leg and can't go on much longer. Him and me snuck away from the others with our horses in the middle of the night when we camped a little way ahead from here. Seaton posted a sentry for the night but he was asleep or wanted to see the back of us because the whole bunch figured we were a burden.

'Both of us need doctoring. There's talk of some Pimas around this way and they have a medicine man but we don't want Indian remedies. Our wounds might go bad on us and even kill us if we don't find a real doctor. And we need grub. We finished the last we had at the stopover at the waterhole.'

'Hand me your gun. Then go back and bring the other fellow and your horses,' ordered Riggs.

Filson complied and began staggering his way back into the midst of the boulders. He re-emerged, leading one horse, accompanied by a second one bearing his injured companion.

Dan Forrest had the look of one almost past caring what happened to him, and he and Filson permitted Riggs and Calland to take their carbines from their saddle scabbards and a Smith and Wesson revolver from Forrest's holster.

'You two are under arrest,' Riggs told them. 'Every man with me is a sworn marshal. Two of them will give you food and take you back to Santa Carmelita. Doc Chivers there will attend to you and you'll be held in custody. The pair of you are pretty used up but don't risk anything smart on the trail or my men will make you regret it.'

Of his deputies, Bill Riggs chose Ted Hawkes, Santa Carmelita's muscular blacksmith, and Harry Trott, another strong man, as the prisoners' escort, and Filson and Forrest were left with them, wolfing food the posse shared with them. Desperate to escape the misery they were enduring on the blazing desert, they appeared to have accepted their fate with docility.

'With those two gone there are five of the Seaton outfit left if the old timer counted correctly,' said Frank Calland as he and Riggs resumed their places at the head of the riders.

'Yes and with Seaton still in command. He's a damned poisonous customer and his whole career shows he's got brains and nerve,' said Riggs. 'He can't be far ahead of us. Unless he's burdened by more wounded, he and what's left of his gang will still show plenty of fight.'

CHAPTER NINE

'THOSE WHO WERE HERE BEFORE'

The posse continued on over the parched landscape as the sun rose to its noon position, beating down mercilessly, causing men and animals to sweat profusely. A little way past the piled boulders, they came across two fairly recent sets of hoof prints leading towards the boulders, clearly those of Forrest and Filson after their desertion from the Seaton party. They were clear guides towards the location of the night camp of the Seaton gang.

Some steady travelling brought them to a point where the tracks merged with those of a larger number of animals of earlier origin, obviously left by the fugitive gang, leading to the location of their camp.

Almost an hour of further travel following the prints brought them to the site of the fugitives' stop-over. It was a place of flat rocks, which the Seaton party had been lucky to find in the darkness. Only yards from a drywash—a sandy ditch-like depression minus any water—it was one of the freak springs sometimes found in the arid wilderness. A tempting small but constant flow of sparkling water issued from a fissure in the rocks.

The boot and hoof-trampled earth around the rocks and some horse droppings spoke eloquently of the very recent visit by a set of horsemen. The Santa Carmelita men settled down for a brief break, replenished their canteens and watered their animals from the spouting spring. They knew that they must now be close on the heels of the remnant of the Seaton gang and each man's vigilance became more acute.

Riggs issued an order forbidding smoking, for they might be so close to their quarry that even the slightest drift of tobacco smoke in the air might give away their presence.

While the party sat on the rocks, slaking their thirsts, Frank Calland noted that Ed Corbett, the intellectual young bank teller, was examining the face of a large, flat rock intently and apparently tracing something on its surface with his finger. Intrigued, he stood and walked over to the young man.

'What've you found, Ed?' he asked.

'Hohokam,' said Corbett. 'Writing of a kind. Very old Indian picture writing. Since the Indians never developed an alphabet, they put messages into pictures. Just take a look at these inscriptions. They're worn away by the wind and weather so you can hardly see them.'

Calland looked closely at the rock face. Scratched into it was a set of severely worn lines which on close inspection could be deciphered as miniature figures of humans and animals. The inscriptions were possibly thousands of years old, the handiwork of a people about whom nothing was known.

'Evidence of the Hohokam, an Indian expression meaning "Those who were here before", the ancient forebears of certain desert tribes,' Corbett said. 'This rock might have some significance to this location. I heard it said that the Pimas are directly descended from the original Hohokam but I guess nobody knows the truth.'

At that moment, the crack of a rifle blasted the air and sent its sharp echoes clattering over the empty land. A bullet zipped past Corbett's head and tore a shard off the rock. Calland instinctively grabbed Corbett's shoulder and forced him to squat low.

'Scramble for the drywash! Get into it, quick!' he breathed as he yanked his Colt from its holster.

There was an immediate surge of activity as the relaxing posse became animated and rushed for their horses to grab carbines from saddle scabbards. All had the same idea and hastened towards the drywash to hurl themselves into it and take up defensive positions on the side facing the direction from which the shot came.

Both Calland and Corbett, having grasped their carbines, and bending low, scooted for the drywash and plunged into it just as another rifle blast shattered the desert tranquillity and a bullet sent a spout of sand into the face of Marshal Bill Riggs, lying with his companions against the side of the drywash.

Riggs spat out sand and mouthed an uncomplimentary opinion of the deliverer of the bullet and he was joined by Calland who, ducking low, hurried along under the lip of the drywash to fling himself down beside Riggs. Both carried their carbines and both wanted urgently to pinpoint exactly where the shooting was coming from.

'From the trajectory of those shots, I'd say Seaton's bunch are on a higher point than us but not too far away,' Calland said.

'That's just what I thought,' Riggs replied. 'There's panic behind those shots because the Seaton mob can't see us hunkered down here, though they could only a couple of minutes ago when we were at the spring. So long as they keep missing, I don't care how much ammunition they spend and they must be running low. Think of the amount they used up at Santa Carmelita and we came out carrying a heap of ammunition and none of it has been used yet.'

'Their numbers have dwindled, too,' Calland said.

'The two we put under arrest said they had no grub. I can't see how they can hang on for much longer.'

As if in answer to that observation with derision, another rifle blast sounded and a bullet whirred ineffectively over the drywash.

'Hey, Marshal, can't we jump out of here and rush them?' called Jack Grover, the gunsmith, eager for action. 'Damn it, there's only a few of them. I reckon we can outshoot them real easy.'

'No, let them waste some more bullets,' counselled Riggs. 'They haven't a chance of hitting us. We can sweat it out here for a spell, and don't fret, Jack, I'm more determined than you are to finish them—particularly that fellow who calls himself either Beale or Daggett!'

Calland, sprawled next to the marshal on the slanting side of the declivity, remembered how Riggs had earlier said he wanted a settlement with the Seaton rider not only for his wounding of Rosemary. Once again, he recalled his earlier impression that there was some link between the two men, hinging on the piece of play-acting Riggs staged when the outlaw fired on him in Santa Carmelita.

'I know you're out to get him, Bill, but I'm not asking why,' he stated, remembering the unstated diplomacy of the West where another man's previous history was held to be highly private.

Another harmless bullet flew over the heads of the

posse, causing the marshal to grin sardonically

'I don't mind telling you—all of you,' he said clearly and firmly. 'That snake is named neither Beale nor Daggett. His real name is Walter Riggs and he's no damned good.'

'Riggs?' echoed one of the posse.

'Yes, and Wal Riggs is my half-brother so I lied to you, Frank, when I said I didn't know him from Adam.'

All the men lying along the bed of the drywash turned their eyes on the marshal, eager to hear more.

'When he was a youngster, he was as good as any man, but the War altered him,' said Riggs. 'I never told anyone in Santa Carmelita about what I did in the War but I fought for the South, though I claim to belong to both the North and the South. I lived a time in Ohio, my mother's state. My father was a Virginian.

'My mother died when I was a small kid and my father took me back to Virginia where he remarried and my stepmother became Wal's mother. Wal and I were close. As a youngster, he was a good, straight shooting character, even though he was reckless and was usually ready to take a chance on anything.

'When the War came, we both signed up with the Confederate army. Wal was Southern born and more devoted to the South than me. He was attracted to Jeb Stuart's cavalry unit. Their hard-riding and adventurous lifestyle suited his devil-may-care spirit from the start.

'Some aspects of southern life didn't sit easy with me but when Yankee troops invaded Virginia, I felt, like the Virginians, that their state had been wronged in a heavy-handed way and Virginia should be defended. I too joined the cavalry but chose a more plodding outfit than Stuart's.

'Wal and I were separated by the War and I learned after a couple of years that he had switched from Stuart's command to one of the dangerous guerrilla units, namely the one commanded by Seaton, then a colonel. He had assumed the name of Beale and some-times Daggett. At least he didn't disgrace the name of our father who was a decent man. I understood he played his part in Seaton's devilment, continuing with him after the War when the whole bunch became thieving outlaws, shaming the honour of worthy Southern soldiers.'

Riggs paused then went on with some bitterness in his voice.

'Wal came into Santa Carmelita to spy out the chances of raiding the bank but I didn't know why he was there. I met him on the street, seeing him for the first time in years. I went to speak to him thinking, stu-pidly, that he might have quit the Seaton bunch. I had the notion that maybe he had reformed but he took off on his horse and fired at me.

'Deputy Calland here saw it all and was for going after him. When Wal shot me, I fell over as if hit to take attention off him. I didn't want him harmed. After all, he was my half-brother. Remembering how he was as a youngster, I still had some hope for him. I didn't want to see him chased and gunned down.'

The marshal shook his head regretfully. 'I know now he had been in the bank and took note of its arrangements for the raid by the Seaton gang. When he shot Rosemary, I changed my view of him. He's as big a polecat as any of Seaton's outfit.'

There was a long spell without any shots from the fugitives and Calland, lying on his belly, slid up the slanted side of the declivity to look at where the shooting came from. He saw a short stretch of desert then a slightly elevated ridge which obviously provided the position for the riflemen. It was within range of the drywash but not high enough to allow a marksman to hit anyone deep in its cover.

All seemed to be quiet but Calland expected the head of a rifleman to show over the ridge at any moment. None appeared. Calland, gripping his Colt, inched forward and boldly showed himself a little more. No reaction came from the ridge. He slithered down into the drywash again.

'There's a ridge out there they were using as a perch but I reckon they moved off from behind it when they found their shots were having no result,' he reported. 'They're now somewhere behind it.'

Bill Riggs thought for a minute, then said, 'With our

horses back at the spring, we'd better go ahead on foot. Their horses must be pretty exhausted, so I guess they can't run much further. We'd best put an advance party forward to see what's over that ridge, then signal the rest to follow if it's safe. Be ready to shoot at all times.'

Calland elected to take the leading group and, with four volunteers, one of whom was Ed Corbett, the young bank teller, slipped out of the drywash, moved ahead to the ridge, mounted it then lay flat to look over its crest.

The whole group gave a collective gasp at what they saw. On an open expanse of desert there stood what looked at first like a huge pile of flat-faced boulders but here and there, the surfaces were pierced by oblong, window-like openings, suggesting it was a man-made structure, an ancient building. It spread over a considerable expanse of the desert floor and, if it was truly a building, it must have had many rooms.

At its base, there was a wide opening like a doorway. Even from the ridge top, the watchers could see the churned tracks of men and horses around the door aperture. There was no sign of any life.

Ed Corbett, who seemed to be interested in the old lore of the Southwest's deserts, gave a low whistle of surprise.

'A mud-house but it's more a palace than a house!' he exclaimed. 'I never believed they really existed outside the tales of old desert rats. They were supposed to be the tribal headquarters of the ancient Hohokam but very few have been found. Nobody knows how old they are.'

Frank Calland felt the stirrings of memories from his days on the New Mexico desert. 'I remember old tales of some such places somewhere out in the wilderness but laughed them off as myths,' he recalled.

He waved a hand, signalling the men back at the drywash to advance.

The remainder of the posse, led by Riggs, emerged from the declivity and ran forward, bending low with weapons in hand. They joined Calland's group, flattened on the ridge top.

'Take a look yonder,' Calland said to Riggs. 'The sort of place the old desert myths tell about. It's the place marked as "Indian ruins" on the map.'

'Well that place is no myth,' said Bill Riggs grimly. 'Those walls are dried mud, thick as those of a fort. Seaton and his crew must be inside, maybe aiming to stage a stand-off from there. They've taken their horses inside so we don't shoot them. Move forward fast, boys. Spread out and head for that doorway. Keep low and ready to shoot.'

The five remaining Seaton gang were inside what was a form of entrance hall to the mud building. It was an eerie, gloomy place where strange designs and pictographs of unknown antiquity were carved into the walls. The intruding outlaws shuddered. Each wished he could take to his heels and flee into the sunlight out of the crushing depression that seized his heart from the moment he entered into the portal of the ancient structure.

The horses of the group were just inside the doorway, brought in from the open as a precaution against the posse appearing and shooting them as a means of stranding the fugitive group and denying them the chance of further flight.

The remnant of the gang hoped they would find the Pimas the old timer told of at this desert structure, but when they shouted into the mysterious darkness behind them, they were rewarded only by hauntingly hollow echoes.

Daggett, Deems and Drago ventured back into the darkness of the long passageway, driven by the vague hope that there might be some source of water in this strange place but, lacking any form of light, they were defeated by the darkness which became deeper the further they ventured into the building.

There was a musty odour pervading the place and the surroundings brought feelings of distinct and threatening foreboding that became more unnerving every second. It was as if some unseen spirit brooded over the very fabric of the structure and threatened a deadly malevolence, creeping from the distant and unknown past, towards the men.

Deems was the first to be unnerved by it. He began to quiver and he felt a chill in his innards.

'I figure this place is haunted. It scares me,' he said in little more than a whisper as if he was frightened of something lurking in the darkness. Even though he whispered, his words came echoing, sibilant and ghost-like out of the cavernous and unknown depths of the passageway.

His two companions, who could not be seen in the blackness, responded in similar unnerved fashion.

'Me, too,' said Drago. 'I feel I'm being watched all the time.'

'And me,' confessed Daggett. 'Let's get the hell out of here.'

They scuttled back out of the darkness to the front of the passageway where there was light at the big doorway and Seaton and de Courcey waiting with the horses, scanning the outside landscape for signs of the posse.

Lack of water and food was telling on Seaton and his four followers, Drago, Deems, de Courcey and Daggett; all that remained of his once feared whirl-wind robbers. Already there had been mutterings about surrender and the eerie, oppressive atmosphere of this strange place, with the realization that the old timer had lied about the helpful Pimas, intensified their jittery apprehension.

Daggett, needing water and sustenance, broke.

Unable to contain himself any longer, he blurted, 'Hell, Jay, we're in a hole here and this is the damndest place to die. I can't see any way of getting out of it!'

Seaton, scowling with his skinny frame quivering, drew his Colt quickly.

'Damn you, Daggett. I suppose you're ready to give yourself up to Riggs and his bunch. I figured you were halfway to quitting ever since Stone Creek City,' he snarled. 'I always had a notion you were yellow right through. With the way you've been acting, you put a jinx on our whole outfit!' He stepped forward, prodding his gun towards Daggett menacingly.

At that instant, de Courcey, close to the entrance, gave an alarmed yell. He saw the posse, afoot, advancing quickly towards the mud building. Jay Seaton and the last of his crew hastened to the portal, lay under it and opened a wild, un-aimed fusillade of firing. The widely scattered posse dropped to the ground, rose as a man then continued to run forward. None had been hit.

The crashing din of the firing by the men under the lintel clattered its echoes into the cavernous blackness of the passageway behind them. Then, mysteriously, a throaty, growling, answering echo issued from the unknown innards of the building. It sounded like the reaction of some untamed, savage beast, rudely awakened from its slumbers in its lair, deep within the building.

Before the outlaw group under the mud lintel could get off another set of shots, there was a grinding sound above their heads and, with dramatic suddenness, large portions of the mud structure, fell down in a cloud of dry dust. Deems and de Courcey were struck on their heads and rolled senseless in the choking dust. Seaton, Daggett and Drago were bowled off their feet, and they fought to stand up and staggered drunkenly, coughing and spitting out the cloud of dust which coated them, giving them the appearance of ghosts.

The fabric of the building, created by an unknown people an unknown number of centuries before, had plainly been disturbed by the concentrated echoing of the shots of the men in the doorway.

Daggett staggered out of the swirling dust, still somehow holding his gun. He almost blundered into Bill Riggs, likewise carrying his big Peacemaker, and was horrified to find his half-brother, who had become a nemesis figure in his mind, was only feet in front of him.

His face was distorted with fury and desperation. He turned his pistol on Bill Riggs with his mouth distorted into a rictus of rage and his eyes glittering madly through its masking dust. There was a savage gurgle behind Daggett and the gaunt and bony Jay Seaton, looking as totally demented as Daggett, came lurching out of the dust, clutching his gun which he swung upward, aiming it directly at Daggett's head.

Daggett turned bewilderedly, realizing he was trapped between the menacing guns of his half-brother and Seaton. Then there was a blast of gunfire which sent an echo off the flat walls of the mud building.

Daggett stiffened, the Colt dropped from his hand and, with a choking sound, he performed a brief, tangle-footed dance, stiffened and fell forward with a hole streaming blood drilled in his forehead. He hit the ground already dead.

Marshal Bill Riggs stood as if petrified, staring open-mouthed at the sprawled corpse of his half-brother, seeming to be gripped by shocked paralysis and oblivious of Jay Seaton, who came forward at a crouch, grinning in a crazy, humourless way. He quickly turned his pistol, still dribbling gun smoke, towards the Marshal of Santa Carmelita.

Frank Calland, immediately behind Riggs, sprang forward with his Colt levelled at the bandit outlaw chief. He felt a dark, almost drunken desire to kill but the sensitivities of a law officer won out. He sobered, and became acutely aware of the need to bring a live Jay Seaton before the courts to make him answer for his long record of crime.

'Back off, Seaton!' he bellowed. 'Back off and drop your gun!'

Seaton looked at Calland for an instant and seemed unable to shoot. Then he heard a noise at the entrance to the mud building behind him. He turned and saw what looked like a chance of salvation.

A frightened, saddled horse, coated in dry dust, was prancing out of the doorway and over the clutter of fallen mud brickwork. Its eyes were wild and it stumbled about uncertainly. The half-stunned animal came very close to Seaton, almost brushing against him. The outlaw, as distracted as the horse and still clutching his gun, rushed towards it.

He presented his back to Calland who wavered and lowered his pistol, unable to shoot a man in the back. The skinny outlaw grabbed the loose rein of the animal and hauled himself into the saddle. He tried to urge speed out of the dazed creature.

Calland hastily holstered his revolver and ran as fast as he could towards the mounted man. Seaton could not induce the horse to move and Calland launched himself at him and grabbed his leg, not yet engaged in a stirrup. He yanked hard and Seaton slithered out of the saddle. He somehow managed to retain his grip on the gun even as he and his attacker fell to the ground and, locked together, the pair rolled and struggled.

Panting and growling, Seaton, sprawling underneath Calland, managed to get his gun arm free and attempted to bring the gun close to Calland's head. Calland flung his arm forward, grabbed the weapon and pulled it from Seaton's grip.

With the outlaw struggling feebly beneath him, he planted a knee on Seaton's chest and trained the muzzle of the gun on his face. A litany of reasons for the destruction of Seaton and his gang whirled through his mind: the many depredations in the outfit's past; the attack at Santa Carmelita; the shooting of Rosemary Riggs; the vindictive exploding of the keg of powder, even the point-blank shooting of Bill Riggs's half-brother seemed to multiply into a sufficient sanction to take the skinny outlaw's life there and then.

Calland sobered for a moment. He remembered the law-star he wore and again, saw that his plain duty was to hold Seaton and ensure that he was alive to be placed before the courts.

He took his knee off Seaton's chest, rose quickly then bent to grasp a couple of handfuls of the bandit's shirt and hauled him upright.

The Santa Carmelita posse crowded around his prisoner and himself. A length of rope was produced and Seaton's hands were bound behind his back. He stood, defeated and scowling at his captors.

Deems and de Courcey, only half-conscious, with Drago, were recovered from the rubble and dust at the entrance to the mud building by the posse and their hands were bound and the posse commenced a mopping-up exercise.

The horse on which Seaton had attempted an escape was calmed and the remaining animals of the Seatons were brought out of the building and pacified after their bewildering experiences.

Seaton and his companions were hoisted into their saddles and the body of Wal Riggs, to give the man known as Beale or Daggett his correct name, was placed over the back of a horse.

Bill Riggs, known for some almost reckless acts of courage as a lawman, watched the process and murmured to Frank Calland, 'I couldn't shoot him, Frank. Even though he was all set to shoot me—I just couldn't do it. It was like the time back in town when he fired on me and I stalled to prevent anyone retaliating. Somehow, I just couldn't see him injured. I guess I always had a faint hope that, someday, he'd reform. After all, he was family and we had great times when we were kids together.'

'That's to your credit,' said Calland quietly. 'Anybody who understands anything about human nature will know how you felt.'

While readying the horses near the opening to the mud house, Frank Calland spotted an object lying in the dust and rubble. He picked it up and examined it with a knowing smile. It was an empty bottle of the kind in which whiskey was sold at army cutlers' stores in frontier forts.

'Army rotgut,' he declared. 'That means the army was here. Probably that bunch of Pimas we heard about was here, too, but the soldiers showed up and hauled them off to the reservation.'

'Too bad,' said young Ed Corbett, standing with a

group of men nearby. 'I've formed a lot of respect for the Pimas. There's a belief they are descended from the Hohokam—Those Who Were Here Before—who were surely an accomplished people and, in their time, a free people.' He jerked his head back at the mud structure.

'Just look at the building they created and you can bet it's not been properly explored inside. And, remembering how that place finished off the last of the Seatons, who's to say the ghosts of the Hohokam didn't have a hand in it?'

CHAPTER TEN

HOMECOMING

The posse, prisoners and a corpse set off on their homeward trek over the desert. They rode without hurrying under a punishing sun, reached the place of flat rocks and the stream with its historic rock bearing age-old pictographs created by the desert ancients.

There, they replenished their canteens, watered their animals and gave them time to crop the modicum of green shoots between the rocks.

They continued their progress, riding through the afternoon and re-connected with the Mexico trail just as the sun's searing power began to be spent, so the monotony of riding the desert flats became slightly more bearable.

They turned their horses' noses for Santa Carmelita and, after ten minutes of progress, a shout from one of the posse drew their attention to a drift of hoof-risen dust some distance ahead of them.

Marshal Bill Riggs called a halt and the riders waited and watched the dust reveal a body of horsemen coming along the trail. They numbered about twenty and they rode in a disciplined fashion, led by a large and heavily bearded man. Even at some distance, it was noticeable that the sun struck a bright gleam off a lawman's star on his buckskin coat.

The men from Santa Carmelita waited for these newcomers to draw closer. The bearded man hailed Riggs as he galloped nearer.

'Howdy! You'll be Marshal Riggs and the Santa Carmelita posse!' he called.

'That's correct, and who might you be?' shouted Bill Riggs.

'Marshal Ezra Jenkins, of Stone Creek City and a bunch of men from our town, at your service,' the other answered, pulling rein as his mount came nose to nose with Riggs's horse. He cast his eyes over Riggs's entourage and noted the scowling and utterly defeated Seaton, and the last of his followers (all with their hands tied and obviously prisoners) and the corpse of Riggs's half-brother, draped over a horse's back.

Marshal Jenkins gave a humourless but satisfied laugh. 'Right glad to see you have that skinny, double-dyed snake Seaton in your hands and I guess these other jokers are all that's left of his bunch. Looks like you did a great job of work, whittling the Seaton crew down to a nubbin.'

'What brings you out here?' asked Riggs, puzzled.

'Your telegrapher, Sim Jones, sent a message through to our telegraph office to say the Seatons had raided Santa Carmelita and raised the very devil, burning buildings and what-all but you folks put up a hell of a defence, kept them out of the bank and they vamoosed, badly licked, with a strong posse on their tails,' stated the Stone Creek City lawman.

'I'm ashamed to say we were caught flat-footed by the Seatons. You probably heard they came in like wild-fire, shot a young bank teller and got away with a heap of money. We sure admired you folks for doing what we should have done, and we figured it was only right to bring out a party to meet up with you and help in nailing the Seaton mob, then maybe give a hand fixing the damage in your town. Some of our boys are trades-men, carpenters and such, and they brought their tools along. Looks like you never needed any help in settling the Seatons' hash, though.'

'No, we managed that chore with some difficulty.' Bill Riggs grinned. 'But we're grateful to you and your men for showing up this way. Turning out on our account was a right neighbourly gesture. Do you happen to have any extra grub with you? We're running low and we have to feed extra mouths with these Seaton prisoners. They're about half starved.'

'Sure,' said Marshal Jenkins. 'Our womenfolk made sure a whole lot of food was made available. Every man was sent off well supplied with rations. We'd be happy to share ours with you. Those damned Seaton specimens can have some, too, to keep them healthy and fit to face the wheels of justice.'

Both sets of riders joined to make an impromptu camp beside the trail. Food was broken out and, for the first time in several hectic hours, the men from Santa Carmelita were able to eat and relax. Marshal Ezra Jenkins, Bill Riggs and Frank Calland conversed about the procedure to be followed with the Seaton prisoners.

'I reckon we can add the depositions for the Stone Creek City crimes to those you prepare for Santa Carmelita,' said Jenkins. 'There are the bank robbery charges and, chiefly, the charge for the killing of young Seth Cooper. Then there are lesser matters like damage to property and endangering the lives of the public.'

'Yes, and when added to the record of the unpunished crimes of the Seaton gang, committed all over the country in the course of their years of rampaging, there'll be a substantial dossier to lay before the courts,' commented Riggs.

Jenkins grinned. 'I have to hand you a fistful of compliments. Your posse did a bang-up job, beating the Seaton gang. Many another bunch would have given up after a few hours. Seems to me Santa Carmelita specializes in devil-be-damned tenacious fighting men,' he said. 'I brought our group onto the Mexico trail, figuring we might either intercept the Seaton gang or meet up with you somewhere. We stopped for water and a rest at the waterhole back yonder, then found tracks of a fair sized bunch riding off the trail into the desert and figured you made them. We were scouting around to find some sign that you'd come off the desert somewhere on this trail.'

The combined riders reached Santa Carmelita just as late afternoon edged into evening. They jogged into the scene of broken and charred buildings around the bank and the marshal's office at the beginning of the town. A lone youth on the street saw the strong body of horsemen with their downcast captives come out of the gathering dusk.

'Hey, folks! The marshal's back and he's got prisoners!' he yelled at the top of his voice.

This caused a surge of life to take hold of Santa Carmelita. Doors opened and, it seemed, the whole of the citizenry spilled out onto the street.

They rushed up to the squad of riders excitedly and clustered around Riggs and Calland. Some wanted to ask questions and others were just curious to look on the bony, somewhat uninspiring figure of Jay Seaton, so greatly feared as a criminal scourge for so many years, as well as the trio who were the last of his gang.

Women were anxious to discover if their menfolk in the posse had returned without injury.

Mayor Amos Cotton forced his way through the gathering crowd to reach the two law officers.

'Rosemary is still at my place and she's doing fine. Doc says she's making a good recovery,' he called to the marshal.

'Thanks, Mayor,' said the relieved Riggs. 'Frank and I will get these prisoners lodged in the cells then I'll come up to your house.'

He, Calland and members of the posse hauled Seaton, Deems, de Courcey and Drago down from their saddles and marched them into the marshal's office. They were lodged in the now overcrowded cells with the prisoners already taken in the assault on the town, including the wounded ones who had been patched up by Doc Chivers.

Leaving them guarded by volunteer marshals and Ezra Jenkins, Marshal of Stone Creek City, Riggs and Calland stretched their legs after their hours of sustained riding by walking up the street to the mayor's house.

They found Rosemary, still in the care of Mrs Cotton, a practical and efficient nurse. She was seated in an armchair with a substantial bandage bulking out of her dressing robe at its left shoulder and her head was bandaged after Doc Chivers's stitching of the bullet crease in her scalp. She was pale but her eyes sparkled.

Diplomatically, Calland stood to one side while

there was a relieved reunion between father and daughter.

Then the girl looked across at him and smiled. 'Deputy Calland, step over here and let me thank you most sincerely for pulling me out of that dreadful mess I got myself into during the big ruction in the town,' she said. 'I was out cold but I understand you put yourself in grave danger, handling that powder keg and in getting to me and hauling me free of the ruckus.'

Calland shrugged. 'Well, it seemed like a good idea at the time,' he said, trying to sound casual. 'I guess I had to show that raw deputy marshals can be of some use sometimes.'

Rosemary quickly became grave. 'Did I give you the impression that I had a low opinion of young deputies? I'm sorry if I did. Possibly, my demeanour was all wrong. Maybe I've always been sort of resentful for staying in Santa Carmelita when I wanted to go to college—even though staying here was my own decision. I hope I wasn't growing into a crabby, frustrated woman though I guarded against it. As for being down on young deputy marshals, well I never was.

'I admit I had experience of only one young deputy and that was nothing special and absolutely nothing important. Young Harry Schultz, who was here before you, certainly had a fancy for me, though I never encouraged him. He was too starry-eyed and a deal too fiddle-footed and fickle for me. In the end, his fickleness won out and he couldn't ignore the lure of the gold rush in Mexico. He packed everything and hit the trail.'

Her mood brightened and she said, 'I learned a thing or two when Seaton hit town. I'm glad I was in that fight. It caused me to win my spurs and to be proud of Santa Carmelita. Now I know I belong here and I learned the full value of the people of the town and I love them all: young, old, pleasant or ornery and cantankerous.' She paused and regarded him with a softer light in her eyes then added, 'And that goes in spades for our gallant young deputy marshal. I recall Dad saying we'd have you over for dinner. Let's make it soon and I'll enjoy doing the cooking.'

Five minutes later, Frank Calland left Bill Riggs with his daughter and stepped out onto the street, now enfolded by the early night.

His heart had not yet descended from the tremendous lift it took from Rosemary's parting gift—her feisty, mischievous and unashamed wink.